The Warrior's Way

JENNA KERNAN

MILLS BOON®

First Published in Great Britain 2017
By Mills & Boon, an imprint of HarperCollins*Publishers*
1 London Bridge Street, London, SE1 9GF

Large Print edition 2017

© 2017 Jeannette H. Monaco

ISBN: 978-0-263-07235-8

Printed and bound in Great Britain
by CPI Antony Rowe, Chippenham, Wiltshire

Jenna Kernan has penned over two dozen novels and has received two RITA® Award nominations. Jenna is every bit as adventurous as her heroines. Her hobbies include recreational gold prospecting, scuba diving and gem hunting. Jenna grew up in the Catskills and currently lives in the Hudson Valley of New York State with her husband. Follow Jenna on Twitter, @jennakernan, on Facebook or at jennakernan.com.

For Jim, always

Acknowledgements

Many thanks to Lt. Christopher Knurr of the Brown County Sheriff's Office for his expertise and advice.

Any mistakes regarding the use of explosives are the author's.

Chapter One

Amazing how much a simple favor could cost you. FBI explosives expert Sophia Rivas waited for her escort to finish introductions. She held her tight smile firmly in place as she shook hands with the chief of tribal police, Wallace Tinnin. The man looked well past the age of retirement, judging from his deeply lined face. He ushered them from the station floor, such as it was, into his small, stuffy office, where everything seemed as old and worn-out as their chief.

Her gaze flashed to the CRT monitor on his desk that looked straight out of the 1990s.

Those things still had cathodes and vacuum tubes inside.

Her escort, FBI agent Luke Forrest, had moved into the office and now gave her a look of warning.

Sophia met Luke's gaze. He was her cousin and the reason she had been recruited into the Bureau. She owed him a lot, but that didn't mean she agreed with him. This entire thing continued to feel like a bad idea.

She opted to remain standing in the chief's office rather than sit in either of the stained chairs facing his overcrowded desk. Chief Tinnin headed the Turquoise Canyon Tribal Police Department, which consisted of nine officers, all male, and one dispatcher, female.

"He should be here soon," the chief assured them.

Who were they waiting for again? Luke told her she'd be working with their best man. Best of nine, she realized. What was his name? Bear Trap. Bearton. Something like that.

With luck he could take her to the reservoir and she could give her opinion and be heading back to Flagstaff by dark. It was midafternoon on Friday and the days were still long. She'd be leaving well after the rush-hour traffic, but would still be heading back to the refuge of her little apartment after the longest week of her life. She usually loved the sanctuary of her place, but this week, on leave, it had become a kind of holding cell, where she paced and obsessed over the review team's findings on her use of deadly force.

Forrest was more than a decade her senior and his short black hair and pressed suit did not hide the fact that, like her, he was Apache. But not of the Turquoise Canyon tribe. They were both Black Mountain, both spider clan, making them kin. They also shared a grandmother, so the connection was especially close. And even though Luke worked in the Phoenix field office, he had heard she was on leave during the investigation.

Had she made a mistake that night, one that could cost her the thing she valued most in this world—her job? No. They would clear her.

She glanced from her cousin to Wallace Tinnin, who moved behind his desk. She wondered why he used an old rusty spur as a paperweight. Had he once ridden in the rodeo? That would account for the limp.

What was happening back in Flagstaff? She knew the protocol because they'd explained it all to her. But she didn't know how long the investigation process would take. "As long as it takes" was not very helpful, but was the only answer her supervisor provided before placing her on mandatory leave.

This was the process. She had to trust it. But she didn't. She didn't trust anything that threatened her job.

Tinnin set down a cup of water before her and asked her to take a seat. She politely declined both.

"Coffee?" asked Tinnin.

She glanced at the well-used drip coffee-maker on his sideboard.

"Maybe just water."

It was delivered in a Dixie cup instead of an unopened bottle. Her smile remained but she cast her cousin a certain look. He seemed to be enjoying himself, judging from the smirk.

The chief opened the top drawer of his desk, drew out a silver foil packet that she recognized was for nicotine gum, popped a white cube into his mouth and chewed. The pouches beneath his eyes spoke of a man running a department that she knew must be understaffed and underfunded.

There was a polite knock and her cousin opened the door. In walked a mountainous man who surveyed the room with a quick sweep before he fixed his stare on her.

"Sophia?" said Forrest, motioning toward the new arrival. "This is Detective Jack Bear Den."

The first thing she noticed—that anyone

would notice—was how damn big he was. Big, tall and broad-shouldered, with a body type very unlike the men she knew from her reservation on Black Mountain. The second thing that she saw was the cut across his lifted eyebrow—not a cut really, but more like a blank spot where a tiny white scar bisected the brow and made him look roguish, like a pirate.

What he did not look like was Apache.

Was their best detective really from off the rez?

"A pleasure to meet you, Ms. Rivas. I'm roadrunner, born of snake."

She answered automatically, giving her clan affiliation. "I'm butterfly, born of spider."

Since the Turquoise Canyon people were Tonto Apache and she was Western Apache, they did not share linguistic roots, so she spoke in English, her second language.

Her brain was still sending her signals that he was not roadrunner or snake or Apache. He did not fit. Did not look like any other

Apache man she had ever met. Still, she extended her hand.

He stepped forward, meeting her gaze. She saw his eyes were hazel with a shift of color toward brown near his pupil, which blasted outward to give way to a true green at the outer rim of his iris. Most Apache men did not have green eyes.

The rest of him was equally appealing, particularly his strong square jaw and welcoming smile, which disappeared as their hands brushed. Tingling awareness zinged from their melded palms all the way up her arm. His eyes glittered and his brows descended. Then he broke the contact as if reconsidering the wisdom of a custom of the white world and not of theirs. He drew back, wiping his palm across his middle as if the touch was somehow dangerous. He left his hand stretched across his flat stomach for a moment, his long fingers splayed on the blue cotton fabric of his button-up shirt. Her stomach did a nervous little flutter as her senses came alive. His fingers were thick with a dusting of hair near each knuckle. His fifth finger brushed the top edge of the silver belt buckle bearing a medicine wheel inlaid in black, red, yellow and white. The four directions, the circle of life, the seasons and a compass to guide a man as he walked through life. Why did he wear that symbol?

Her attention dipped below the buckle and stayed fixed long enough for the room to fall silent. The detective's hand shifted toward his personal weapon. Holstered at his hip was a .45 caliber. Then his hand dropped to his side, at the ready.

They'd taken her Glock for the investigation and offered a replacement weapon—a .45 caliber, just like his. She didn't like the stronger recoil. It affected her aim on multiple discharges.

Tinnin cleared his throat and motioned Jack forward. He took a position near her, in front of the desk between Tinnin and Forrest, in only three strides.

Her hand continued to tingle as if she had touched the hot wire of a horse pasture.

She wasn't attracted to Jack Bear Den. She couldn't be. She didn't mix business with pleasure and she wasn't planning to stay one minute more than it took to deliver the bad news.

All three of them were now staring at her. Had they asked her a question?

"What's that now?" she said, her voice sounding odd above the constant buzzing in her ears.

Tinnin fielded that one. "I said, we would like you to advise us on where we might be vulnerable. Specifically, how to protect the reservoirs above us."

"You're on low ground. No protecting you if any of the dams blow." She gritted her teeth as both Tinnin and Bear Den exchanged glances. She should have thought before she spoke.

The councilors told her that she was bound

to feel some anxiety after the shooting and that she would question her own judgment. They hadn't even a clue at how this investigation was messing with her. She was usually way more thoughtful.

"I'm sorry. I spoke out of turn," she said.

She met Bear Den's steady gaze. Her skin felt clammy as the stirring sexual desire crashed against her determination to avoid entanglements. If she'd met him in a different place and time, maybe. But he still looked dangerous. Some part of her liked that, but not the part that liked to eat. Protecting her job meant keeping things professional. What would they say at headquarters if they heard she'd used her leave to bed this guy? Her stomach tightened in dread.

Sophia glanced away from temptation, past the window and the dusty venetian blinds. It was a fine bright September day. The air was cooler at this elevation and it made her homesick for Black Mountain. Everything was green now after the annual monsoonal rains and those, too, reminded her of home.

"I'm sure I can make some useful suggestions," she said. Suggestions like recommending they all move to higher ground if they believed the threat was viable.

She looked to the yellow-and-white rock face that rose on the far plain beyond the flowing water. The Hakathi River threaded through the wide plain. This land, even this office, had once been river bottom. But that was before the dam had captured the water—before the government stole this land and then gave it back to the Turquoise Canyon people.

Bright September sunlight glinted on the glassy surface. The placid winding river didn't fool her. It was dangerous, the vanguard of what lay above their settlements.

"Will that be all right, Sophia?" A man's voice snapped her back to attention. It was Luke who had posed the question.

She lifted her brow at Luke in a gesture that

she hoped would alert him that she had not heard a word.

Luke steepled his hands together as if preparing for prayer. "Sophia has been in all the recent briefings, but the Bureau did not put forth your theory. I think it would be of benefit to share it now."

She agreed with that. And listening to their problems sure beat worrying about hers. The minimum administrative leave was five days. But she was already past that. Was that bad? And when exactly would they give her the "pertinent information" they promised her? Last she'd heard the autopsy was complete. When would they release her weapon?

"Yes, I'd appreciate that," she said as she turned to the chief, but she could not resist another look at the detective.

His hair was short, dark and thick with a definite wave. She'd like to rake her hands through that hair.

Chief Tinnin pushed the gum to his cheek, placing it there like chewing tobacco.

"Ms. Rivas, our tribe isn't convinced that the threat of the eco-extremist group BEAR has been neutralized by the death of their leader, Theron Wrangler."

Her office had gone over this in a briefing before the shooting. During the devastating wildfires in July, a prominent citizen and eco-advocate had been murdered. Suspicion had been cast on his wife, Lupe Wrangler, but no evidence was found and she was cleared.

"We feel BEAR is alive and well and that our reservoir system is a likely target for attack."

BEAR was the acronym for Bringing Earth Apocalyptic Restoration. In layman's terms, they wanted to blow man back to the Stone Age, where he couldn't destroy the planet. Some part of her believed man was the earth's biggest threat. But she was no eco-warrior.

Luke surprised her by revealing information she felt proprietary.

"The FBI believes that the death of Theron Wrangler has crippled their organization," said Luke.

Bear Den took it from there. "A member of our society witnessed Lupe Wrangler shoot her husband."

Luke rubbed his forehead and then picked up where Bear Den had left off. "We could find no proof, no evidence to support this man's claim that Lupe Wrangler killed her husband."

Bear Den broke in, his voice now containing a dangerous edge. "Her daughter also witnessed the shooting. You have two witnesses."

"Nonetheless, the Bureau could not break Lupe Wrangler's alibi."

"She should be in custody," said Tinnin.

"I agree and I'm here doing what I can." He had his hand on his neck again, massaging away the tension that now crackled in the room.

"We believe the witnesses. It's not over."

She now recalled the theory that Wrangler's death might trigger sleeper cells to action. Could these men be right? She decided to proceed as if the threat was viable, as she had been trained to do, until she knew otherwise.

"Tribal Thunder contends that this is not over," said Jack Bear Den.

"Tribal Thunder?" she asked.

"These men are Tribal Thunder." Luke motioned to Tinnin and Bear Den. "It's the warrior sect of their medicine society."

She knew about medicine societies—mostly that they were misogynistic groups, all male and secret as heck. Sophia looked from one to the other and speculated on their activities. Certainly protecting their people would be their prime objective.

"Just a few ground rules before you two visit the dam." Tinnin pinned her with his eyes—he no longer looked tired, but was rather deadly serious. "You will be with one of my men at all times."

Her gaze went to Bear Den. It was him, of

course. She knew it and the prospect excited and terrified her.

"Detective Bear Den will escort you."

"That's not necessary."

Tinnin glanced to Luke and then back to her. "Your cousin wants assurances you are protected because of the recent incident. He and your supervisors feel there may be an ongoing threat."

She doubted that. Sophia glanced at Bear Den. He looked capable, but an FBI agent did not need the protection of a small-town cop.

"Detective Bear Den is very good and knows the territory," said her cousin. "He's an ex-marine. Weapons specialist. He's been a tribal detective for seven years here and knows the terrain. He is an honored member of his medicine society, the Turquoise Guardians, and of the elite warrior society, Tribal Thunder. He's their best."

Best of nine, she thought.

"You can trust him to keep you safe."

Bear Den spoke to her and his voice was deep and rich as dark coffee. She loved the sound.

"My honor," he said.

She cast him a dubious look and he inclined his chin, as if readying for a fight.

"Detective Bear Den will make sure you are safe," said Luke. "It's a condition of your consultation."

"My supervisor onboard with this?"

"He had no objections."

She blew out her frustration. "Fine."

"So you will have protection 24/7," said Tinnin.

"Maybe twenty-four. Certainly not seven. This won't take as long as you think," Sophia assured him. Her confident smile was met with silence. "I'd like to get started."

Because the sooner they started, the sooner she could get out of here.

"Detective Bear Den will bring you up to the

closest reservoir now," said Luke. Bear Den cast her a wicked smile.

And that was when it happened. Her body, always reliable, and her mind, always predictable, both short-circuited at once. Her stomach flipped as she squinted at him trying to figure how the upturning of his lips could make her go all jittery inside. She met the steady stare and the challenge with a smile of her own. The connection grew. He had an air of confidence and a physicality that inspired her to all kinds of bad ideas.

"Check in with me tonight, okay?" said her cousin. "Let me know when you expect to be finished your consultation and I'll come get you."

She tore her gaze from the detective.

"Sure thing," she promised.

"We'll make sure she stays in touch," said Tinnin.

He handed her a large boxy black Motorola

radio that looked a decade old. She clipped it to the waistband of her slacks.

"You ready for a tour?" asked the detective.

"Absolutely. I look forward to it." She didn't, because the idea of being trapped in a vehicle with him made her skin itch.

Chapter Two

"Agent Forrest said you were on leave. But he was unclear why you were on leave."

She glanced at him cautiously, perhaps recognizing a fishing expedition when she heard one.

"Was he?" She made no excuses and offered no answers.

He snorted at her posture. Jack Bear Den slowed his stride to match that of his charge. Sophia Rivas was a beauty, but she wasn't very big, reaching only to his shoulder.

She looked straight ahead with her chin up, as if nothing bothered her. Well, *she* bothered *him*. Had certainly gotten under his skin in record time.

Jack accelerated to reach the passenger side door of his SUV before she did. She increased her speed and then let him go. He had the vehicle door open when she reached him.

She looked younger than thirty-three, with wide dark eyes that shifted to scan the vehicle's interior before she cast him a dubious gaze.

"Is that your mobile data terminal?"

The laptop was old and looked like it had been kicked down a flight of stairs, but it worked. Mostly.

"What about it?" He knew he sounded defensive. The FBI had all the toys and nearly unlimited resources, and he'd had to fix his side mirror with duct tape.

"Nothing," she said, wisely closing her mouth.

Her gaze met his and locked in like a sniper zeroing in on her target.

For a moment he saw the trained FBI agent instead of the most appealing woman he'd seen in…forever. He was just dying to know why she was on administrative leave. He was also dying to know what she looked like naked, but that was an incredibly bad idea. He'd been assigned as her protector. It was a sacred duty and nothing came before his duty.

She carried no weapon at her hip. So she preferred a shoulder holster beneath her blazer. He couldn't see it, but could see just a little honey-brown skin at the modest scoop of her collar. His higher vantage allowed him to also see the slope of her breasts. He glanced away, placing a hand over his own service weapon, which was clipped in a leather holster to his belt. You had to rock it backward to get it clear. Most folks wouldn't know that. But Sophia Rivas sure would.

She glanced at his hand, his thumb locked under the belt just before his weapon. Then her gaze swept up over him in a way that made his entire body flash between alertness and sexual arousal. Finally her gaze held his. She had big amber eyes framed with dark spiked lashes and the kind of mouth that made a man do stupid stuff.

Oh, no. This was not happening. He was not having sexual fantasies about a woman who looked at his headquarters, vehicle and person with a cool disdain.

How had she ended up in explosives? Forensic explosives expert. Odd choice, that.

He reached for her elbow to assist her and she gave him a certain look that made him hesitate.

"I can make it," she said and climbed into his vehicle. He moved to close the door, resisting the pull to step nearer to her. Then he rounded his SUV and slid into the driver's seat.

He wiped his damp palm on his trousers before turning the key. He gave a cough meant to clear his dry throat.

"Thank you for agreeing to help us."

"I'm not sure how much help I can be. The canyon walls are steep on both sides and we are clearly in a gap in what used to be river-bed."

"You wouldn't want to be here if any of the three reservoirs go."

"Can we tour the interior workings of the dam system?"

"Yes. I've arranged a tour for tomorrow."

She gave a little laugh and shook her head.

"What?"

"My cousin knows that we aren't seeing the interior until tomorrow?"

"Yes, I mentioned it to him."

"And yet he sent me up here today. Where is it I will be staying? I didn't see a hotel or casino."

"Yeah, we don't have a hotel, or rather we do and it is connected to the casino, but it's being renovated. Grand opening is this November. Maybe you can come back."

"I highly doubt that."

"Don't worry, I have a bed for you."

Agent Rivas was out of the car and marching toward the station before he could turn off the ignition. He didn't see her again until he reached the squad room and that was only her back as she entered his chief's office without knocking.

He slowed as Olivia, their dispatcher, gave him a look.

"I wouldn't," she advised.

He took her advice and waited. It didn't take long. Rivas emerged red-faced and panting, her fists clenched. She cast him a murderous look and continued past him. He let her stride away, following until he returned to his seat beside her in his SUV.

"Ready?" he asked.

"Not even close," she said. "Why didn't you tell me that we would not be alone?"

"You didn't really give me a chance. It's on our tribal gathering grounds. There are several cabins. I'll be there along with some of the members of Tribal Thunder. But you'll have a private cabin. It's a beautiful place beside the river and we have a lodge with a generator for gathering at nights."

"Nights? I only packed an overnight bag. You think there will be more than one?"

"Tinnin said we'd have you until Tuesday. Time enough to see all four dams, inside and out."

She rubbed her slender neck and looked straight ahead. "Four days. After that I'm going home, even if I have to walk."

They sat in silence, the A/C blowing in their heated faces. The air between them seemed to move with currents all their own. He hadn't felt this kind of attraction, ever.

"Can I call you Jack?" she asked.

"Sounds fine. Shall I call you Sophia?"

"Fine."

"You want to know why I'm stuck up here in the hinterland instead of working on a case?" she asked.

Jack shifted in his seat. "Sure."

"I was involved in an incident of fatal force."

That was a euphemism that told him she'd killed someone. Likely shot them.

"I'm sorry to hear that."

"So I'm on administrative leave until they finish the investigation and clear me."

"FBI conducts their own investigations, right?"

"Yes."

"So you should be fine."

"What's that supposed to mean? You think they'll sweep any mistake I made under some rug bearing the FBI seal?"

He shrugged and set his vehicle in motion.

"Well, they won't. I could be relieved of duty, permanently. And that can't happen."

"If you say so."

"And they wanted me to see a shrink. When I said no, they extended my leave.

"It wasn't even the assignment I'm working, which is going to hell, I'm sure. Luke thought

I might like to go home to our rez." She shook her head. "Can't do that so he came up with this to distract me. A welcome diversion. Ha. Oh, anyway, it doesn't matter. I'm stuck here until they take me back."

"You can't go home?" he asked.

She cast him a look and then turned to stare out the window. Only then did he realize he had asked Luke nothing about her upbringing. All he knew was that she was of the Black Mountain people, butterfly born of spider.

But who was she deep down, where it mattered? Jack wanted answers.

"You want to talk about it—the investigation?"

She shook her head.

"Okay. I'm a good listener. Just saying. So, do you have brothers and sisters?"

She didn't look at him. "Yeah. And tons of cousins. My mom came from a big family. Where are we going?"

"Top of the canyon. I thought I'd give you an overview. Okay?"

She nodded.

"I've got three brothers," said Jack. "Carter is the oldest. He's my twin and he's coming home soon. He's under protection by the Department of Justice."

That sure got her attention. Her posture changed and she half turned to stare at him.

"Why?"

"Witness. He went with his wife, Amber, who survived the mass shooting at Lilac copper mine. She was going to testify in a federal case against Theron Wrangler."

"But Wrangler is dead and so they don't need witnesses."

"That's right." She was quick and pretty.

"Then there are Tommy and Kurt. They are younger. Kurt flies in the air ambulance out of Darabee. Next town over. And Tommy is a Shadow Wolf on the border."

"Border patrol?"

"They work under Immigration and Customs Enforcement—ICE. But he works with border patrol, too."

"Shadow Wolves. That's the all–Native American outfit, right?"

"Exactly. They're on the Tohono Oodham lands."

"I've been down there. It's hot."

"Most of Arizona is."

"But not here and not Black Mountain." She seemed to have lost some of her bristle. "Listen, I'm sorry your people feel threatened by BEAR."

"What's your take on it?"

"I'm not briefed. Really, I only know that group has been connected with the Lilac shooting and might be involved with the Pine View wildfire in July."

On the drive he told her what he could. Carter had rescued Amber Kitcheyan from the Lilac copper mine and placed himself between her and BEAR's assassins, and the Lilac shooter had been caught. She knew that the mass murderer had been subsequently executed and that the assassin was a member of the Turquoise Canyon Apache tribe, Detective Bear Den's tribe. She did not know that the shooter had been terminally ill, or that his death had brought suspicion on his daughter, Morgan Hooke.

"Our men set up protection for Morgan Hooke as a precaution."

"What happened?"

"She helped us recover the blood money paid to her dad. And she and her daughter are safe. You'll meet Ray Strong soon. He's one of our men and her assigned bodyguard. Soon he'll be her husband."

She made a face that showed her disapproval of that turn of events.

"You know about Meadow Wrangler?" he asked.

"More than you do, I'd suspect."

"She witnessed her father's death."

"I know that. I also know she has a history of substance abuse resulting in rehab."

"She got drunk at eighteen and swam in a country club's fountain."

"She's an unreliable witness."

"We believe her."

Sophia shrugged. "Your prerogative."

They crested the top of the canyon rim and Jack brought them to a halt.

"This is it. From here you can see Skeleton Cliff Dam above our land and also Piñon Forks and Koun'nde, our two main settlements. Turquoise Ridge is out of sight and also above flood level."

"Let's have a look." She exited the vehicle and their doors closed simultaneously.

Jack walked easily to the edge of the rim, where the rock bluff ended, leaving the dizzying drop to the valley below. The river had once cut this canyon from solid stone and spanned the gap where the town of Piñon Forks now stood. He had never seen the river roar with the yearly monsoonal rains because the dam and reservoir system had been installed in the 1920s, long before the stretch of his memory. But the old ones remembered. Few had seen it tumble and rage and then shrink like the belly of a woman after giving birth. The floods left rich fertile soil deposited yearly. They also left wetlands that burst with mosquitoes and that brought yellow fever. Crops were raised in the rich earth, but now the land was fit only for grazing livestock and none died from yellow fever. Was it better now than before the river was tamed?

He didn't know. He only knew it was different. They had electricity, mobile phones and no crops.

"That's quite a drop," she said.

"Nine hundred meters from that point above us. Over a half-mile deep." Jack smiled. "See that spot over there?" He pointed to the arched cut in the yellow sandstone. From here it looked close to the water. "That's just short of eleven meters—higher than an Olympic diving platform. We used to jump off it into the deep water."

"That's foolish."

"Fun. It was fun."

"You and your friends sound reckless. I don't take such chances."

"Too bad. It was a thrill. What did you do up on Black Mountain for fun?"

Her eyes went sad and then she looked away, leaving Jack to wonder what kind of a childhood she'd had on her rez.

"So what do you want to show me?"

Back to business then. He pointed out the landmarks, towns and road system along the river and bridge east of the reservation. Beyond sat the great gray wall of Skeleton Cliff Dam that allowed just enough water to keep their livestock alive and their towns above the waterline.

"That looks like a very healthy vein of turquoise," she said, motioning to the line of blue threading through the canyon wall beyond the river.

"Yes. It is good quality, too. We don't mine by the river anymore. Too much overburden," he said, pointing to the dangerous overhang of rock created by undercutting the hill to retrieve the turquoise below. "But we have some nice veins farther north at Turquoise Ridge. Very hard and nice nodules. Turquoise varies by looks and quality. That over there is brilliant blue with a webbing pattern called 'bird's eye.'"

"I know it."

"We also have bright blue with flecks of iron pyrite up on Turquoise Ridge. That's our main mining sight now. It's pale blue to dark blue. We get a little green sometimes. But that's rare."

"You wear it on your belt," she said.

He tilted the buckle. "Yeah. This is from that ridge," he said, grazing a thumb over the brilliant blue outer inlay that surrounded the medicine wheel. Then he lifted his hand to brush the grey Stetson on his head. "My hat-band, this paler blue with the fleck of black chert matrix, this is from Turquoise Ridge."

"Chert?"

"Those are the blackish inclusion of the host rock that makes the cut stones more valuable, similar to spider web veining. Some collectors prefer the veining and inclusions to the solid blue stone."

"You know your turquoise," she said.

"Major biz here. Digging it, selling it at the rock-and-mineral shows. We go as far as Australia for shows. And we make jewelry." He looked back over the rim to the blue river of turquoise that threaded through the dark stone. He pointed. "We derived our name from that vein of turquoise. It would be a shame to cut it all away. We do collect what erodes and you'd be surprised."

He followed the direction of her gaze as she glanced from the mineral vein down to

Piñon Forks and then returned her attention to the opposite rim a mile up from where they stood, pausing on the yellow rim of rock. This was the narrowest section of the canyon. Here the walls became pinched so the canyon was wide enough only for the river that touched the cliffs on both sides. He always thought that this spot must have been a heck of a rapid before the dam.

He tried to picture the surging torrent that once climbed far of the smooth walls and hoped he'd never see the water forced through that narrow gap.

Now her attention flicked to the wide flood plain, where his rez had placed their major settlement, Piñon Forks, then lifted to fix on the Skeleton Cliff Dam.

"That is really close," she said, folding her arms before her. The gesture lifted the tops of her breasts so that he saw the mounds of firm tempting flesh over the scoop of her maroon blouse. His mouth went as dry as the cliff stone.

She turned to him and opened her mouth to speak, then caught the direction of his stare. Her hands dropped to her sides. Her amber eyes and sinking brows sent a clear message of displeasure.

"Sorry," he said.

"I was about to say that the reservoir system in total is at a high-water point for the year. August rainfall set a new record and so a break in any of the dams would theoretically compromise the one below. If I was trying to destroy the system I would focus on Alchesay Canyon Dam because it's the largest and holds back Goodwin Lake."

"Your cousin told us that the FBI presence is focused on that dam as well. But what if they hit this one? Skeleton Cliff Dam is very close to our land. It wasn't even land before they dammed this river."

"Listen, with the force of that water and the

speed, I have to be honest. If the dam goes, there would not be time to evacuate. And that break would carry enough water and debris to at least overflow Red Rock Dam below your lands. Likely Mesa Salado Dam, too."

"That one is above the Yavapi Indian Reservation."

"It would shut down the power grid for Phoenix." Her hushed voice relayed the gravity of her thoughts.

"Your cousin told us he can't discuss the surveillance methods on the dam system, just that they do have eyes on all the dams, have taken preventative action and established rapid response for various scenarios."

"We do our job, Jack."

"So what steps do we take?"

"Other than evacuate all low-land areas indefinitely, I can't really offer suggestions." She waved her hand toward the opposite rim. "Your best hope is to protect the dams."

"They aren't our dams. We can't protect them."

"We're protecting them."

Jack sent a look her way that he hoped relayed his lack of faith in the government protecting his people—history was on his side on that one. She rolled her eyes, returning her attention to the flood plan.

"Evacuate now," she said.

"We have nowhere to go." She made a face. Then she shook her head and her voice took on a sarcastic edge. "Well, you could blow up that entire ridge up there. That would stop anything. Theoretically."

He'd never considered fighting an explosion with another one. But it could work.

Her eyes rounded. "Jack, it was a joke. Just a stupid offhanded remark. You can't blow up that canyon wall."

"I can't. But you could."

Chapter Three

"That's crazy. I'm not blowing up anything. I'm here to advise you," said Sophia. She was sweating now, but it was a cold sweat and her skin had gone to gooseflesh.

One thing she knew with certainty—there was no way in hell she was ever, under any circumstances, doing anything that could affect the outcome of her fatal force investigation. Destroying federal land in a massive unauthorized explosion qualified.

"No," she said. "No way and hell no."

Jack's smile told her that this wasn't over and she felt like kicking herself for opening her big mouth. What if they did something incredibly stupid, like tried to blow that opposite wall and then they told her supervisors that it was her suggestion?

"You can't be seriously considering this." She tried to make her voice reflect her incredulity, but instead there was a definite tremor.

"I'll consider anything that keeps my people from drowning."

"We're protecting the dam system, Jack. You and your warrior society don't have to do anything. This is federal land. All of it. It falls under federal jurisdiction."

He pointed toward Piñon Forks. "That's Apache land and we will protect it as we see fit."

"I hope you like federal prisons, because that's where you're heading if you blow one single rock of this canyon. This is a wetland system. It's crucial to the power grid and it's beautiful."

"You have a better idea?"

"That wasn't an idea! It was a joke."

"How would you set the blasts, in your joke?" he asked.

"You must think I'm crazy to answer a question like that. Besides you don't have access to the kind of explosives you'd need."

"We have mining explosives, det cord, blasting caps and rolls of shock tubing."

He used the abbreviation for detonation cord, used to trigger explosions of the main charge and his knowledge caused her to lift her brows in surprise. "Turquoise mining," he said, answering her unspoken question. "The community operation is mostly underground now, following the veins as they run deeper. Plus we have lots of smaller claims. My friend Dylan Tehauno has a really good one up there on Turquoise Ridge. Lots of blasting material here."

"If you are considering this, I have to report you."

He smiled as his eyes challenged her. "Just a joke. Like yours." He glanced toward the west. The town below was already cast in shadows, but up here it blazed orange as the sun made its final descent.

He sat on the canyon rim and glanced up at her. "Want to watch the sunset?"

She sat beside him, close enough to feel the heat of his body but not quite touching him.

"Turns the river into a ribbon of gold." He pointed to where the river flowed a deep orange color that changed by the minute.

"Jack, I'm in the middle of a fatal-force investigation. I cannot be involved in blowing anything up. This is a consult. Remember?"

"Back to the investigation again. Why are you so worried? Did you screw up?"

"No. I—well, I don't think so. Maybe."

"You can tell me, Sophia."

She lowered her head, staring at nothing that he could see.

"I'm a former US Marine. I've shot people before."

"That's different." She waved a dismissive hand. Then squared her shoulders and drew a breath. She was going to tell him and the realization filled her with both hope and terror.

"Do you know that there is not one person in my office that has even discharged their weapon, let alone been engaged in a significant-use-of-force incident? Well, Mel drew on a pit bull but he didn't shoot because he got over a fence in time."

"It happens to a lot of us," he said again. "And if you can't sleep or think or eat, that's all just part of it. The crappy part, but it's necessary. Eventually, you live with it. Mostly the memories stay down."

He sat beside her overlooking the river as the clouds changed colors before her eyes. *Clouds*, she thought. That meant more rains would be coming.

"I shot a young Hispanic male," she said.

He nodded. Saying nothing but somehow his silence encouraged her to continue.

"Here's what happened. I'm going to say it fast so I don't have to think about it all night."

She drew a breath as if preparing to submerge in deep water, then let it out. "Okay, I was off-duty and in my new car. I had just leased a BMW, black, Two Series. I mean I just left the dealership and I got bumped. I considered that it was a scam and so I had my weapon out when I left the vehicle. The male driver told me to step away from my BMW. Actually he said, 'Give me the keys.' And then he called me a...well, it doesn't matter. He demanded the keys and reached for something in his coat. I saw the handgun before I fired. He died at the scene."

Jack scratched his chin, feeling the stubble growing there. Seemed like a home run to him. She'd defended herself and from her version he saw no reason for her to worry.

"Seems justified."

"But it wasn't a handgun. It was a phone. He did have an unregistered handgun on his person. But that was not what he pointed at me.

And he kept the phone pointed at me, even when he went to his knees."

"You think he meant to photograph the damage?"

"I'll never know."

"Sophia, he told you to give him your keys. There is only one reason to hit a new Beamer and then demand the keys. He was boosting your car."

"Probably."

Jack's anger took him totally by surprise. He tried to understand why he was so furious at this unknown perp. And then it struck him. He'd be murderous with anyone who threatened her. How had she gotten under his skin so fast?

She could have died and he would never have had a chance to know her. He wanted that chance. Trouble was, she didn't. She had made it very clear that she could not wait to be out of here and back on the job.

"Does he have a criminal record or history of stealing cars?"

"I don't know. They won't tell me anything, and I don't have access to the system. I do know his name. Nothing else yet. I've made my formal statement. I met with the union rep and our attorney. They gave me the protocol."

"Referral to mental-health professional?"

"Sure. And contact with an agent who also had a deadly force encounter in Phoenix. But he was on a raid of a grow house and everyone inside was dirty and heavily armed. Not the same."

A grow house was a home, usually abandoned, taken over and converted to an indoor greenhouse to grow marijuana. The drug producers were often well armed and prepared to defend their crop.

He said nothing. No one's life experiences were the same, but all could be used to help every person find their path.

The silence stretched as the first star, Venus, appeared in the western sky.

"They've been investigating since Sunday. SAC said he'd keep me updated. He really hasn't."

"SAC?"

"Special agent in charge. He's my liaison to the thirteen-member SIRG. That's 'shooting incident review group.'"

"Really?" Thirteen seemed like overkill. But this was the FBI. He knew that their investigation would be exhaustive and in-house.

"I haven't heard anything since Thursday, when he told me the autopsy had been completed and that I should get my personal weapon back next week."

"Any results from the autopsy?"

"He's still dead."

Jack almost laughed, but reined it in. She looked so grim.

"So what's next?"

"Interviews with the two witnesses. Photographs. Diagrams and the report by the administrative director of the office of inspections."

"That's a real thing?"

She cast him a scowl. "Of course. He's chairman of SIRG."

"Supervising the cast of thirteen."

"Twelve, minus himself."

"I can see why you're nervous."

"No. You can't. Your shooter had fired at you. My shooter was pointing a camera. One of the witnesses also had a phone and may have taken a photograph or video."

"More evidence."

"Yes."

"You feel you made a mistake?"

"No. But what matters is what SIRG thinks. If they rule my actions unjustified, I could lose my job. Everything."

There was a definite note of panic in her voice.

"All the schooling, training, work...gone."

She snapped her fingers. "Like that. And I'm not going back…" Her words trailed off.

Back where? To her reservation? He cast her a questioning look, but Sophia had clamped her mouth shut and laced her fingers so tightly in her lap her fingernails were going blue.

Jack offered her the only thing he could think of. "You have his name. I can run him through our system."

Her eyes shifted to him.

"You'd do that?"

Jack didn't say so aloud, but he'd do a lot more than that for her because despite knowing that she could not wait to put him and his tribe in her rearview mirror, he was desperately attracted to her.

"I would."

She wrapped her arms around her knees and rocked back and forth. He lay a hand on her shoulder and she stilled and glanced up at him.

"Thank you." She placed a hand over his. It

wasn't until her hand slid away that he could breathe again.

"Yeah. Don't mention it. Name?"

"Martin Nequam."

Jack asked for the spelling and she provided it.

The light had changed again, casting the sky in bright fuchsia and red. He glanced away from her, taking in their surroundings.

"It gets pretty dark up here at night," he said. "And the road can be tricky. We'd best head down. Get you settled. And I want to introduce you to the others."

She followed him back to the SUV. "What others?"

"The men of Tribal Thunder, Dylan, Ray and my brother Kurt. Carter, when he gets home. And Ray's wife, Morgan."

"You're not talking about the daughter of the man who murdered the Lilac gunman?"

"The very same. Also Dylan's fiancé, Meadow Wrangler."

"*The* Meadow Wrangler? As in, daughter of the murdered prime suspect and leader of BEAR."

"It's her mom. Even Meadow says so."

"Interesting attack team. You have at least two members who might be working for BEAR."

"They're not."

Sophia got back into his vehicle and clipped her seat belt, saying nothing to that. She would not be offering any more advice and she would sure as heck not be making any more jokes.

"You wanted to be sure we weren't alone."

"So instead we have a party."

"Planning committee."

"If you really feel threatened, then they should be planning an evacuation."

They drove along the road that was more switchback than straightway. The angle of descent was jarring and Sophia had to hold on to the handgrip above her passenger window to keep from jostling into Jack Bear Den, whose wide body spilled across the center console and into her personal space.

She was not sure what to make of him. He was a detective, sworn to protect and serve. Did blowing the opposite ridge qualify? Only if he was right and the dam failed. But then there would be no time to set the charges. They would have to be placed early.

Why was he so darn big? She was attracted to big, muscular men. Jack unfortunately ticked all the right boxes except for one—he was trying to get her mixed up in a career-ender. She'd worked too long and hard to get off the Black Mountain rez to jeopardize that. Having a career gave her money, respect and purpose, and it kept her from having to ever rely on the system to protect her.

He held the wheel as he flexed his arm muscles and stretched, showing thick fingers nicked with white scars on the knuckles in the golden light of sundown. He had strong hands to match the rest of him.

Sophia liked men, but she didn't depend on them. She glanced at Jack, his face now cast in shadows as they crossed below the line of sunlight. Sleeping with him would be dangerous, but perhaps the thrill would be worth the risk. As long as she remembered that after she toured the dam system, she was out of here and he was not coming along for the ride.

Jack angled his head and shoulders, making his joints give a popping sound, without ever releasing the steering wheel.

"We'll be down soon."

The road did finally level out to a rolling pasture. He flipped on his headlights. They continued through the town. She glanced at the tribal headquarters, which had lights illuminating the great seal of his people. It featured the river, of course, the cliffs and a single sacred eagle above them both.

They continued downriver as the sun set, and drove past the neat houses and fences that held the cattle. Cattle, ranching and rodeo were all a way of life for her people as well. Signs warned to watch for horses.

"You don't pen the horses, either?" she asked.

"No. The river and canyon does that," said Jack. "We're just up here." He slowed and turned onto a dirt road, lined with barbed wire on each side. She could see the cattle, dark shapes in the fields. The headlights made their eyes glow green as they passed.

She lifted her phone and called her cousin, checking in as he requested. But she didn't tell him about the misunderstanding about her flippant suggestion which the detective seemed to be seriously considering.

Jack pulled off the main road and drove toward the river again.

"This is the place where our medicine society gathers. It has a large outdoor meeting space, sweat lodge and fire pit. But most importantly for you, the tribe uses it for ceremonies, so we have several cabins on site. You'll have a one-bedroom with working bathroom. Hot and cold water, too. I'll take the one beside yours. Ray Strong has the one on your opposite side and Dylan Tehauno the one after that. Ray's wife, Morgan, and her girl will be here for dinner, then she's got to get their daughter back home. Lisa is Ray's stepdaughter, actually. But Meadow Wrangler will be spending the night. Couldn't keep her away."

"I see."

She was about to say that it wasn't necessary for the others to chaperone. But the way he looked at her gave her pause. He seemed hungry and that simple glance was all it took for her heart to pound and her stomach to twist. Oh, she wanted Jack Bear Den in all the ways a woman wanted a man. And since she could not leave, having chaperones might be a really wise idea. She needed to either stay away from Jack or get it over with. After all, he was just a man. Getting him out of her system might be the wisest course. There was no regulation against sleeping with him. He was not a colleague or a suspect. He was the friend of her cousin.

Fair game.

Sophia ignored the internal warning alarm sounding in her mind. She'd had short affairs before. They were the best kind, allowing her the excitement and physical contact of a man's company without the entanglements. Leaving before they did was just self-preservation, because, sooner or later, they all left. But she'd never been this interested before. In fact, she had intentionally picked men she had minimal interest in. Made leaving easier.

"Sophia? Will that arrangement work for you?"

"Seems fine, but not Wrangler. She's connected to an ongoing investigation. It would be best if I had no contact with her."

"See, I'd think you'd want contact. Especially if you think she's involved."

"Not my investigation," she said.

"We don't think she's involved."

"Why is she still up here? I'd think a woman like her would be bored to death."

"Well, if she leaves, the highway patrol or Flagstaff PD will arrest her as a person of interest in the Pine View fire."

"Ah," said Sophia.

"She didn't do it. But you make up your own mind. If you don't want her to stay, I can speak to Dylan. But it's an insult and he's my friend."

"They're a couple?"

"Yes, but they don't live together."

That surprised Sophia. From all accounts Meadow was a wild woman with numerous short, public affairs.

Sophia took the irresistible bait to meet the infamous heiress, Meadow Wrangler.

"She's your guest," said Sophia.

He gave a toot on his horn and hit the lights of the SUV. A moment later the headlights illuminated a large square structure, the lodge she supposed. Onto the porch spilled five men, two women and a child. She recognized only one—Wallace Tinnin.

"That's our tribal director in red. The rest are all members of Tribal Thunder."

"The men, you mean."

"No, all. Our warrior sect includes women. But not children. Lisa, the girl, is not yet a member. But if we are successful, she will live to join someday."

The gravity of his words struck her. What for Sophia was a hypothetical problem to be considered and quickly set aside was for the Turquoise Canyon Tribe a matter of life and death.

Jack made introductions on the porch. Sophia shook every hand as if she was running for public office. She recognized Meadow Wrangler from her photo, but the blue hair was new. Sophia tried not to stare. When she met the executive council president, she both shook his hand and bowed her head in respect. She did the same when she met Kenshaw Little Falcon, their shaman and leader of their medicine society.

The formalities complete, Morgan Hooke offered to take Sophia to her cabin to freshen up.

"Where's Agent Forrest?" asked Sophia.

Kenshaw Little Falcon took the question.

"He had to return to Phoenix. I drove him to the airport in Darabee. But he left the car for you." He motioned toward the dark portion of the field, where she had seen the vehicles parked when they'd arrived.

Luke had abandoned her. Nasty trick, she thought. Sophia tugged at the hem of her blazer and forced a smile. She was now alone among strangers.

"I see."

Morgan lifted a lantern from a nail and motioned Sophia down the steps.

Sophia knew of Morgan since her cousin had been lead on the FBI investigation into the shooting of the Lilac gunman. Morgan's father had killed the shooter, a paid assassin, according to Luke. How had that affected this woman and her child?

"Let me show you to your cabin so you can freshen up before supper," Morgan said again.

Under the bright starlight, they picked their way to the cabin. Morgan preceded her through the door and set her lantern on a small wooden table. Then she fished in her pocket for a book of matches, lifted a second lantern from a nail beside the cabin door and lighted the wick. The smell sent Sophia right back to the home of her childhood, making her stomach roil.

"Everything all right?" asked Morgan. "It's not much, but Dylan cleaned it up and Meadow changed the bedding. It's all new."

Meadow changed the bedding? The woman she believed to be a spoiled little rich girl had made a bed? Sophia couldn't believe it.

"Meadow?"

"Yeah. She's not so bad."

Oh, Sophia had to disagree. If she wasn't

bad, she lived in the same house with bad for most of her life.

"It's lovely," said Sophia.

And it was so much nicer than her childhood home on the Black Mountain rez had been.

"Well, you can't beat the view of the river and the canyons across the way. You can't see it now, but tomorrow, from the porch, it's beautiful."

The river again. It seemed to be taunting her now.

"Plumbing works. Hot water, too. Just no electric. You know how to light a kerosene lamp?"

Sophia was all too familiar with how to do so, but had hoped she would never have to use a lantern again.

She forced a smile. "Absolutely."

"They brought your bag in. It's by the bed."

Sophia followed the direction Morgan indicated and found both her briefcase and the bag Luke suggested she pack "in case things run long."

"Do you want me to wait for you and bring you back to the lodge?" asked Morgan.

"I can find my way."

"Well, I'll leave you to get settled."

Sophia just wanted to slip into her yoga pants and a loose T-shirt and climb into bed. It had already been a long day.

"I'll be over in a few minutes."

"Bring a lamp," said Morgan as she hesitated at the door. "We are so grateful to you for coming to help us. Luke told us all about you, and we are hopeful you can give us advice so we can protect ourselves. I don't know if Jack told you but I lost my father to cancer. But before that I lost him to BEAR. It's a dangerous group and none of us believe they are done. They still have the Lilac explosives. If this is their target, we are in terrible danger."

Sophia did not have the first idea how to reply. Mostly she felt guilty for wanting nothing more than to get out of here. Being so close to the river now gave her the creeps. And she realized why. Because she believed her cousin and Morgan. BEAR was still out there. How would she feel if she could not pack up and leave in four days?

Had they planned all this, Luke and their shaman, Little Falcon? To show her the pastures that lined the river and the town and this gathering place, the very heart of the reservation, so she could see what would be lost? The problem that had been theoretical was now all too tangible.

Morgan hesitated, lingering. "I have a little girl. We live right in Piñon Forks. Her school is there, too." Morgan's hand went to her stomach and Sophia saw the definite bump she had not seen before. Morgan was expecting a child.

The two women stared across the silent cabin.

"I'll do what I can," said Sophia.

Morgan cast her a sad smile and left her with

her troubled thoughts. For the first time in five days, the investigation was not the most important thing on Sophia's mind.

Chapter Four

Sophia unpacked, then used the bathroom, checked her hair and reworked her ponytail before heading back across the open ground with the darn kerosene lamp held high to light her way.

She knocked and entered. The smell of fry bread made her mouth water and brought her back to some of her earliest memories. Meadow motioned her to a chair and the group sat to eat baked chicken with a tangy sauce, mashed potatoes, corn, three different types of casseroles, including one of a noodle pudding that was especially good, and the fry bread, golden brown and piping hot. Sophia knew how much trouble it was to turn the simple ingredients for fry bread into dough and appreciated the effort as much as the flavor.

After the meal, several newcomers arrived and both Morgan and Meadow were absent. Their shaman greeted her formally, as if they had not just shared a meal, his smile flanked with vertical lines. Then he motioned her forward to meet an older man, who wore his hair cut blunt at the shoulder. About his neck was a bolo of the tribe's great shield inlayed with stone. The river, she noted, was a fine blue spiderweb turquoise.

"Sophia, this is our executive director, Zachery Gill." The older man extended his hand as Kenshaw continued speaking. "Gill is the new leader of our tribal council. Zach, this is field agent and explosives expert Sophia Rivas."

Gill had a fleshy tanned face and was dressed simply in a cotton shirt and jeans with no indication of his rank outside the ornate bolo.

"Welcome to Turquoise Canyon, Agent

Rivas. Thank you for answering our call for help," said Gill. He motioned a broad hand to the empty chair and she took a seat. Gill sat to her left as everyone took their seats. The circular dining table had transformed into a war room.

Each attendee introduced themselves by clan, family name and first name, and ended with their position. They were tribal law enforcement, tribal council and warriors of Tribal Thunder.

When Jack spoke her stomach fluttered and she mentally scolded herself for her very physical reaction to the man that was seated on the far side of the table, which she now realized resembled a medicine wheel with each section made from a different color of wood. Jack sat at one point and she at another of the four directions. Did he notice that the line bisecting the table seemed to connect them?

Finally the circle came back to their shaman. Kenshaw rose as he addressed the gathering.

"Some of our tribe have been elected to protect the language, some care for and teach our young people, and still others guard our heritage. These men and women have one mission, the survival of our people, and each and every one is prepared to defend our tribe with their lives. They are at your service, Agent Rivas."

"While I appreciate the offer, no one is going to die as a result of my visit. I'm just here to have a look at the reservoir system. I'll report back to my field office if I see any gaps in their existing protective plan. I can assure you that no one is going to compromise the power grid."

There was a general shifting of chairs and postures. You didn't have to be a master at reading a room to know that the tribe members here disagreed.

Director Gill spoke to Sophia. "Jack was just telling us about your plan to create a makeshift dam with a series of controlled blasts at the narrow point of our canyon."

Her eyes flashed to Jack's and held. "That was not at all what I advised."

Gill continued as if she had not made an objection.

"We feel, that should the Skeleton Cliff Dam fail, we would not have time to evacuate our people."

"I can assure you, it is very safe, protected by our Bureau and the state highway patrol."

"Yes, we know. We have seen them and our warriors have gotten past them. Back to my point—if the dam was to fail, how long would we have to evacuate?"

Gotten past them? That wasn't good at all.

"That would depend on the scale of the breach."

Gill lifted his thin brow at her. "Total breach."

She drew a breath and released it. There was no way to deliver hard news but directly.

"Minutes," she said.

JACK WATCHED SOPHIA'S face as she delivered the news that the two settlements along the river, Piñon Forks and Koun'nde, would not have enough warning to evacuate.

"But they could be moved to higher ground now. You have three towns. Those in the lower two could move to..." She lifted her gaze to the ceiling as she tried to retrieve the name of their third and smallest town.

"Turquoise Ridge," Jack said.

She smiled at him and his stomach trembled in a way that he hadn't experienced since middle school, when all his hormones had been popping in different directions. He grimaced. The woman was near desperate to be clear of them all. He knew that, but still he could not deny that, even knowing she couldn't wait to be rid of him, he was still imagining what she'd look like out of that suit.

"They could relocate there," said Sophia.

Zachery Gill took that one. "We have only sixteen hundred members. Over nine hundred live on the rez, nearly all of whom live along the river. Turquoise Ridge is for our miners and loggers. There's nothing up there but rock and ponderosa pine."

"But it's high ground," she said.

"It's impossible. We even asked FEMA for temporary housing. I'll bet you can guess the answer."

Judging from the pressing of her full lips, Jack felt that she did. FEMA would not provide emergency housing before an emergency and the federal and state officials had indicated that all was safe regarding the reservoir system.

"Did you say you got men past the security?" she asked.

"Men and women. The road across the top of the dam is blocked with one concrete barrier on each side and a state police vehicle on the east side. We were allowed on tours with only our tribal identification cards and saw the inner workings of each dam during public tours. We were allowed to walk up to the top of the dam."

"Single individuals could not carry enough explosives to destroy a dam. At worst they'd damage the power station."

"We have a twenty-four-foot police boat, which had been seized from the property of a drug dealer convicted on their rez. We use it for water rescues and search-and-rescue."

He had her attention.

"We were able to bring it and a flat fifteen-foot Zodiac with a load capacity of 250 pounds simultaneously within ten feet of the base of the dam. We were there nearly forty-five minutes before there was a response."

Sophia was no longer meeting the director's gaze. Instead she was staring into space. A moment later she reached for her phone.

"I need to check in."

"You're on leave," reminded the shaman.

"But if what you say is true then I need to report this."

Zach smiled. "We tell you this for two reasons. One, because we wish you to see that we are vulnerable."

They waited but Zach said no more. Sophia glanced at Jack, the look of confusion evident. He did nothing but glance back to the executive director. But now there seemed to be a steel band around his ribs squeezing away the air from his lungs and making it hard to draw a full breath. If just looking at her did this to him, he really, really needed to avoid touching her. Yet he could think of nothing else.

Sophia inadvertently rescued him by directing her expressive dark eyes at Gill.

"What is the other reason?"

"You are here and you are listening."

"Yes, but I can't help you blow up the canyon. It would be an ecological disaster for the river, not to mention destroying the water supply to both Red Rock and Mesa Salado Dams below this position."

"We disagree," said Kenshaw. "Creating a

temporary dam of rock and debris would actually save both dams from the flood and debris that would at best test the limits of their infrastructure. All reservoirs are at their limits now after a record rain. We believe this is what BEAR has been waiting for. The rains have come and gone and the water is high."

"I can't help you do this." She folded her arms. The action lifted her breasts.

Jack stared and when he finally tore his gaze away, it was to meet Ray's knowing glance. Jack wanted to knock the smirk off his face. Ray had settled down since marrying Morgan and taking on the role as father to Lisa. They were now expecting their first child, but there was still devilment in him. Ray leaned toward Dylan Tehauno and whispered something. Dylan's gaze snapped to Jack, and he stared with wide eyes full of surprise. Jack had a reputation for being very selective when it came to women. Jack shook the thoughts from his head and realized Kenshaw was speaking, his voice as hypnotic as the wavering notes of a flute.

"No need to decide and no action to take. Tonight we will pray and dance and perhaps then know better what direction to go."

"Folks will be arriving soon," said Gill to Sophia. "You are welcome to join us. Tomorrow Jack will take you to the reservoir system. You can see if you think the protection is adequate. After that we will talk again."

Sophia stood. "Then if you'll excuse me, I think I will turn in. Early start tomorrow."

Actually they would start late. Jack wanted her to see the day tours, but also night surveillance because Kenshaw was right. It was not that hard to get past one state police car parked at one end of each dam. Closing the bridge spanning the dam was a predictable security measure. But one Humvee followed by a tractor trailer could knock the concrete barrier aside without even slowing down.

There were many things Jack wanted to

show Sophia Rivas. But he would stick to the ones relating to the reservoir system. For now.

Jack followed Sophia out of the council lodge. He paused to grab her kerosene lantern. The lantern was unnecessary really, because of the waning moon, now in its quarter. The silvery light reflected back on the placid surface of the Hakathi River.

"You forgot your lantern," he said and offered her the handle.

She made a sniffing sound. "I don't like them."

"Lanterns?"

"Yes, lanterns—they smell," she said.

"I like it—it smells like—"

"Poverty," she said, finishing his sentence.

He cocked his head at the odd association. Did she mean that people used kerosene when they had no electricity? For him the association of the lantern brought back memories of camping along the river as a boy, but perhaps she did not have electricity in her home on

Black Mountain. His tribe had some homes on propane up in Turquoise Ridge, but most everyone had electricity and septic tanks. Hadn't she?

"Well, we don't need it. It's bright enough."

She just kept walking until she reached the front porch facing the river. All the cabins faced the river so he understood why she had picked the wrong one. Close, just one off, but this was his cabin for as long as she stayed with them.

"Um," he said. Should he tell her or let her figure it out on her own?

She rounded on him. "You had no right to take an offhanded comment and present it to everyone as if I had suggested blowing up your reservation as a viable option."

"Seemed like a plan."

"It's a disaster. It will ruin the canyon and it will boomerang back to me. Your little stunt in there could cost me my job."

She worried about protecting her career

while he worried about safeguarding the lives of everyone here.

"It wasn't a stunt, Sophia. I'm trying to save my people."

"That's *our* job—the FBI's. And we can do our work more efficiently without a bunch of lunatics performing a ghost dance and then blowing themselves to smithereens."

The ghost dances had been used in a vain attempt to remove the scourge of white men from the west by the Sioux people, who followed the great spiritual leader the Anglos called Crazy Horse. His real name was *Tȟašúŋke Witkó*, which literally meant "His Horse is Crazy." But Jack understood the reference. Their shaman called for all the people to come and pray and dance tonight. Like Crazy Horse, Kenshaw Little Falcon believed in the old ways. But he also honored the new. In other words, pray but also act. Her comparing his tribe's gathering to the ghost dance was both insult and honor.

"How about you wait until tomorrow to see what you think of the job the authorities are doing?"

She stiffened and placed a hand on the latch.

Behind them the string of headlights marked the arrival of the tribe, as they wound along the river road like a great, brilliant snake.

On the great open area between the main lodge and the cabins, the central fire was being lit.

"Are you sure you won't come?" Jack motioned to the gathering place. "I'd love to watch you dance."

"I haven't danced for a long time." She sounded wistful.

Dancing was a form of prayer for their people, a way to communicate to the great divine while still connecting to the earth.

"You could just sit on your porch and watch. Then come join us if you like," he said.

"Maybe." She pulled the latch and the door

cracked open. She regarded him now, really looking up at him.

He went still under her inspection, hoping that she liked what she saw. His nostrils flared as he tried to bring enough air to sustain him, but each breath brought her delicate floral scent to him. He breathed it in, making it a part of him. He swallowed but his throat was still dry. He was looking at her mouth now, thinking what it might be like to kiss her slowly at first and then...

"I'd better go," she said.

"Sophia?"

She stepped closer. Oh, boy. He was about to tell her that she was at the wrong door, but maybe it was no mistake. Maybe she knew exactly which cabin this was. That thought made his wiring short-circuit. His blood rushed and his breathing quickened as the desire drowned the rational part of his mind.

"Yes?" She brushed the tips of her fingers down the center of his chest.

"This isn't your cabin."

She stepped back. Damn, he should have kissed her first and then told her. But then he might not have wanted to tell her. Not when his bed was only a few short steps away.

He wanted her in that bed more than he had wanted anything in a long time.

Car doors slammed and headlights swung into the field they used for parking. Voices reached them as the people began to gather.

Sophia looked around her. "Which one is mine?"

Jack pointed and watched her go. He didn't follow. Not just because he was needed in the drum circle, but because they needed Sophia's help. Kissing her, sleeping with her, might make it easier to convince her. But it also would lead to the bloody same questions women always asked.

Why don't you look like your brothers? Why are you so big? Have you ever thought about speaking to your parents?

Jack let his hand trail over his wallet. Inside were the answers. But he just couldn't bear confirmation that his mother had deceived his father and he was the visible sign of that infidelity. Everyone suspected. No one spoke about it. Except the women he dated. That seemed to make them feel they had some right to turn him inside out. It didn't. Never had. Never would.

Chapter Five

Sophia stood on the porch of the little cabin and listened. The men sat in a circle around a huge drum, each with a leather-tipped drumstick, collectively beating the rhythm for the dance. She could see them all by firelight and recognized many; Ray sat next to Dylan, who was beside Kurt Bear Den. Then came three men she could not see because their backs were toward her. Adjacent to them, Jack Bear Den sat in profile. He was a full head taller than any of the others and that was while he was sitting down. His appearance raised all sorts of obvious questions. The investigator in her wanted answers. But the part of her that kept her own secrets did not.

Much of her childhood had been horrific and blocking it out just made sense. No different than blocking someone on social media. Except those drums. They brought back something she hadn't remembered, the good part. Belonging to something bigger than herself. Walling herself off, avoiding going home, it was logical but now she felt a longing that made her weep.

So here she stood, leaning against the porch rail and watching the Turquoise Canyon tribe dance in unison around the central fire. Her head bobbed in time and her feet shuffled from side to side. She knew this dance, knew the meaning and the purpose.

There in the light of the fire went Morgan Hooke and beside her was the Anglo Meadow Wrangler. She did not seem to care that she was an outsider, as she matched her steps perfectly to the others. Sophia studied Meadow and how the other women reacted to her. From Sophia's perspective, it seemed that this tribe accepted the heiress despite her outlandish ocean-blue hair and relations with the known head of BEAR. Sophia longed to join them but something kept her rooted to the porch. If she were similarly welcomed, it would be harder to leave.

She wiped away the dampness on her cheeks and straightened. It didn't matter. She didn't need to move in slow harmony around the fire or sing the songs to earth and sky. But a prayer might help the outcome of the internal investigation. A song sung with so many voices was a powerful thing. Was it strong enough to give her back what was taken…her badge, her gun, her position?

She needed them. Needed to be away from here and back where she belonged. On the job.

Sophia sang softly to herself. The song was a prayer, her tiny voice mingling with the people. Their languages were different. She hoped it wouldn't matter as she returned to the language of her youth, her terrible wonderful youth beside the high black-capped mountain. She sang the next song as well and was still there when the logs fell inward and the drums went silent. Still there clinging to the porch rail when the gathering broke and the engines of the cars and trucks started. She watched the vehicles cruise away. Saw Jack Bear Den lift the drum as big as a truck tire and carry it single-handed into the lodge.

She retreated to the shadows as his friends made their way to their cabins. Ray chased his new wife past her door as Morgan giggled like a girl.

Next came Dylan and Meadow, strolling arm in arm, their heads inclined so they touched. They paused at the river and shared a long kiss that was so full of love and desire that Sophia had to look away. She turned toward the lodge and saw Jack Bear Den standing before the steps leading to the cabin beside hers. His eyes were pinned on her. The shroud of darkness wasn't cover enough to keep him from locating her.

"You didn't come," Jack said. His voice was low and only for her. Had he been watching for her? That thought made her tingle all over.

She glanced over at Dylan and Meadow and was surprised when Meadow kissed Dylan good-night and then retreated alone through the doorway. Sophia blinked in confusion as what she knew of Meadow's wild reputation for men and parties clashed with the chaste kiss. Dylan walked alone to the next lodge and vanished inside.

"They don't?" Sophia asked.

Jack shook his head. "Nope."

"But why? They are clearly in love."

"Because to marry her is to give Meadow federal protection from the local wants and warrants regarding the wildfire. Meadow won't have the people thinking she married

Dylan for that reason. Someday, she will marry him. When the matter is settled."

"That could be years." Sophia looked at the dark lodge. Beyond the window Sophia thought that Meadow must be preparing to sleep in her empty bed. "It could be never."

"Her choice," said Jack. "And a difficult one. But one that has earned her much respect here."

Sophia returned her gaze to Jack, taking in the readiness of his stance and the way he was now angled away from his cabin and toward hers.

"I was hoping you would join us," he said.

"I did not want to intrude."

"We want you here, Sophia. Everyone. And they want to meet you."

"I won't be here that long."

He nodded. "More reason."

"You want to sit awhile?" He motioned to the bench beneath the single window on his porch.

Sophia knew with certainty what would happen if she crossed the distance between them. It wouldn't be sitting.

"Detective Bear Den, I want you to know that I'm not in a relationship at present."

His brows lifted at this change of direction.

"By choice. I like men, I just don't like them encroaching, you know, on my space. I need privacy."

"I wouldn't think I'd be encroaching for long. Like you said, you're leaving."

"Yes."

"Just as well. I need my space, too."

She was so tempted to walk right over to him and lace her hands behind his neck and kiss him with everything she had. That's what she wanted. But it wasn't wise.

"I'm not getting mixed up with you," she said, narrowing her eyes at him.

He walked to her porch, placing one large foot on the bottom step as he gripped the rail and broke into her personal space.

"If you say so."

She backed toward her door.

"If you change your mind on the encroachment thing, you know where to find me."

Men were like that, just like stray cats. But they didn't stay. Not for long, and a woman who was wise knew to take care of herself. Relying on a man was a lot like working with explosives. You kept clear if you could and if you couldn't you wore protective gear.

"Good night, Detective."

"Good night, Agent Rivas." He followed her with his eyes. "Did you hear me singing to you?"

She had—his voice was low and deep and distinctive. He'd sung one full song alone. It had made her insides ache.

"Was that for me?"

"Couldn't you tell?"

Sophia stopped backing away and took one step toward him. He was up the steps in an instant.

"I just want to kiss you good night," he said.

"One kiss."

His arms went around her and she felt the restrained strength as he leaned her back. She angled her head so their mouths met. The touch of his mouth was firm and enticing, the contact quaking through her like a shock wave. That had never happened before. If she was smart she'd pull back. Instead she wrapped her arms around his neck and pulled him closer.

Jack moved toward the door, opening it with one hand as he swept them in a slow circle until they stood inside. The kiss that he'd planned had gone quickly off the rails. Sophia's response had left no doubt that she felt the burning want with the same fierce intensity as he did. But as soon as they were inside, she pushed back. He resisted the silent request for release for just a moment and then let her go.

He held back the curse and only just kept from reaching out to reel her back in. It couldn't end like that, half-finished with both of them panting and unfulfilled.

"Sophia, there's no reason not to. You and I aren't colleagues. You're here as a favor to a friend."

"I'm still a federal agent on leave awaiting an investigation."

"This, what is between us, has nothing to do with that. It won't impact the investigation in any way. You're hurting and worried. Let me comfort you, help you forget all that."

"I don't sleep with men I've only just met."

He nodded. "You just kiss them silly."

"You kissed me. I did say one."

That was a qualified no. Perhaps she needed to know more about him before trusting him. He could do that. She wasn't staying and he was trustworthy, as long as she didn't start up with the same hard questions they all asked.

She had not yet asked. Surprising for an investigator.

"So what is it you want, Sophia?"

"I want to see the reservoirs and get back to Flagstaff, back to my job and my home and my life."

"But you felt it, too, Sophia. I know that was no ordinary kiss."

"We'll talk about it in the morning," she said.

"Talk. Sure. We can talk." Not happening, he thought. "Breakfast in the lodge in the morning. Coffeepot in there if you are up before seven. Good night, Sophia." He didn't turn until he reached the porch. If she was still in there or if she closed the door then he'd know she wanted no more from him. But if she followed him…

He turned at the edge of the porch. She was in the doorway, one hand on the latch and one on the frame. Sophia wanted him. She just didn't want to make a mistake. Jack smiled. She wouldn't be here long, but time was still with him.

"See you in the morning."

He could feel her watching him. He paused

before his door, facing her across the distance that separated them.

"You know where to find me." Jack stepped inside and closed the door, leaving the bolt open. She wasn't going to follow him. But she was going to think long and hard about what would have happened if she had.

Chapter Six

Of course, Sophia couldn't sleep. The minute she set her head on the unfamiliar pillow, the worrying started. She went over her initial interview in her head and then her formal statement. The special agent in charge had looked at her so strangely when she had declined to call a family member the day of the incident. What was so odd about that? Lots of people had no family. Only she did have some. Her mother and sisters and brothers, some of whom she did not remember or had never met. Five days mandatory leave. Two weeks until the investigation had to be completed. Eight days before a ruling. Everyone said she shouldn't worry. They'd rule she'd been justified. But if they didn't she'd be referred for a disciplinary review.

She could smell the wood smoke though the open window. She glanced out at the side of the adjoining cabin and the open window. Jack's window.

Now she couldn't sleep because she was thinking about that kiss and his big warm body just next door.

Sophia rolled to her side, giving the window her back. If only she could just lie next to him and tell him everything. That would make her feel better, wouldn't it?

Thinking about it sure didn't help. She sat up. If she walked over and then just asked to talk…

Sophia thumped back on the mattress. If she crossed his threshold, it wouldn't be for pillow talk. It would be for the kind of comfort a man gave a woman. Her body hummed, preparing for him even as she kicked at the covers and pounded the pillow.

Tomorrow they would see the reservoirs.

The flute music intruded into her thoughts. It was so low that at first she thought it was in her mind. But then she knew that it came from the cabin beside hers. Jack Bear Den—that giant of a man—was playing his flute for her. And just as in the old legends the music made her heart beat faster and her eyes grow misty. Was he wooing her or was this what he did before sleeping?

He was awake. She rolled to her side and propped her head on her hand to listen. She didn't mean to fall asleep, but the music was so sweet, each note a reflection of his breath. She breathed with him and soon slipped into slumber.

She woke to a birdsong and blinked her eyes open, disbelieving that she had slept the entire night. She hadn't woken once. That had not happened since the incident.

Sophia sat up and glanced toward the open window, smiling. He'd given her comfort without touching her or intruding or asking for a thing.

It did not take long to wash up since there was no shower, just a sink. She dressed in a different blouse, but the same trousers, donning her shoulder holster and then her blazer. Outside the sun blazed, streaking across the floor of the single room and heating the cabin.

A new fragrance wafted through the open window—coffee and bacon. She took a moment to fix her long hair in a knot at her nape. She had packed limited cosmetics, but did apply a tinted gloss to her lips and used the liner and mascara before slipping into her shoes and heading out.

Kenshaw Little Falcon sat on the porch and was the first to greet her, first in Tonto Apache and then in English, inquiring as to how she slept.

She was cautious of him because Luke had

told her of the shaman's involvement in BEAR. He was a federal informant, but also possibly an eco-extremist with a long history of activism.

"I slept well, thank you," she replied.

"It's the river. The sound of the water is very soothing."

The river. Sophia pressed her smile into a tight line as she continued into the lodge to find three men crowded in the kitchen. There was Ray, Dylan and Jack.

Morgan was nowhere to be seen, but Meadow sat alone at the table with her coffee. She offered a bright smile.

"There she is," she said.

This brought all three men around. Jack cast her a dazzling smile that made her stomach tighten.

"Coffee?" asked Ray.

She nodded. "Black."

He grinned. "Do all law personnel take their coffee black?"

"I believe it's regulation," she said.

That made Jack laugh. The sound vibrated through her insides and made her skin go to gooseflesh. Their eyes met and held. His mouth quirked and his eyes sparkled. Was he thinking about the kiss?

As if in answer, his gaze dipped to her mouth.

"Help yourself," said Dylan, motioning to the counter that separated the circular gathering table from the kitchen. "We have eggs, bacon, fry bread and grits."

Her gaze turned to the fry bread. Her mother didn't often make the Apache staple, but when she did, it was fine. Her mouth began to water and she took the plate Dylan offered. She joined Meadow and wondered if she should keep the conversation light or try to find something useful about the eco-extremist group her parents ran.

Jack joined them first, leaving Ray and Dylan to manage the kitchen.

"How did you sleep?" he asked. His warm smile shone on her like sunshine. She wanted to scooch her chair closer just to be nearer to him. Instead she lifted her coffee mug in salute.

"Well, thank you. When will we be leaving?"

"Soon as you're ready."

She focused on her breakfast, pausing only for a second cup of coffee. Meadow finished first and left them alone at the table. Dylan and Ray had begun to argue about the importance of using butter versus oil in cooking. The discussion quickly changed to light-hearted insults.

Jack motioned his head toward the two men. "They always do that."

"Most men do."

He sipped his coffee and the act of pursing his lips made her go all jittery inside. He lowered the mug.

"Something wrong?"

Really, really wrong. Wrong time. Wrong place. And wrong man.

"Nothing at all. I enjoyed your flute playing. Do you always practice at night?"

"Naw. That was for you. I've been in a deadly force encounter, Sophia. I remember the investigation and I remember not sleeping much. I'm sure it's more formal at the Bureau. But they still put me on leave. I hated every minute."

She was staring now. He'd been where she was.

"Will you tell me about it?" she asked.

"Sure. On the way to Skeleton Cliff. Okay?"

"That'd be great."

"Anything more?" he asked, motioning to her empty plate.

Had she eaten all that fry bread? Generally her morning repast was coffee and yogurt mixed with flaxseed. This was better.

"Yes." She stood and took her plate to the

kitchen, where Dylan relieved her of it. "Great fry bread."

He looked pleased. "My mother's recipe. Few ingredients, but lots of work."

Pulling and stretching the dough. She remembered because she'd learned how to make the staple with her mom. Seemed they always had flour, salt, milk and shortening, even when they had nothing else.

"Delicious," she said.

"You shouldn't eat fry bread," said Dylan. "Too much fat and carbs."

"Listen, there is nothing better than carbs for energy. It's what we run on."

"It gives you diabetes," said Dylan.

Jack touched her elbow and motioned with his head toward the door.

She let him drive. He flexed his fingers and then gripped the wheel, waving at Kenshaw as they left the compound.

"You have enough air?" He fiddled with the direction of the vent. "Usually ride alone."

"I'm fine. So…" she began, trying to sound casual, and watched him brace himself. "You were in an officer-involved shooting?"

His shoulders relaxed. What had he thought she was about to ask?

He chuckled. "I thought you might ask about that, but I was hoping…"

"What?"

"You'd ask me if I was seeing anyone. I thought after last night you might want to know that."

"It was just a kiss."

"Was it? To me it was more."

"So. Do you have a girl?"

"Currently unattached."

"The same. Most men aren't very understanding of the hours I keep."

"I hear that."

His smile lit up the compartment and made her insides squeeze. Her cheeks went hot and she had to look out the window at the river to catch her breath.

"So..." she said, bringing the conversation back to safer ground. "About the officer-involved shooting."

Chapter Seven

Jack didn't like to talk about it. Every law enforcement officer knew the risks. Knew they might die on the job. But most didn't really consider the impact a deadly force encounter would have on the rest of their lives.

"First off, I was a US Marine. I saw action in Iraq and lost a good friend there. Dylan, Ray, me, my brother Carter and Yeager Hatch all joined up together. I almost lost my brother and Ray. Hatch didn't come back. We miss him all the time."

"I'm sorry. I've never lost a colleague."

"He wasn't a colleague. He was Ray's best friend and the five of us were inseparable."

"Yes. I see."

"We were attacked by insurgents. I wish I could say that I felt something for the men I killed over there. Mostly I still just feel anger. But the deadly force incident was different. I knew them."

She sat in quiet attention as he continued driving along the river and into Piñon Forks.

"There was a warrant out for the driver. I pulled him over and found he had a passenger. His kid brother, Donny, was eighteen. They were both dressed all in yellow and black."

"Yes?" As if she wasn't sure what that signified.

"You don't work gangs then?" he asked.

She shook her head. "They don't use explosives, generally."

"Yellow and black are the gang colors favored by the Latin Kings."

She nodded her understanding. "What was the warrant?"

"Skipped on his hearing. Used Donny's 18

Money to make bail and then pulled a no-show."

The accumulated per-capita dividends from the tribe's revenue sources, including their casino, was called 18 Money. She'd used her own 18 Money to get out. The funds were enough to pay for her education, her first apartment and a very old Toyota. Her mother expected her to turn the money over to her for her use. When she didn't, her mother threw her out.

"I had both of them out and had the driver cuffed when Donny pulled a gun on me. I wish I could say I saw it coming, but I didn't, and he got a shot off before I drew my weapon. They never found that bullet, but his gun had been fired so all clear on that. I hit him three times in center mass. He was wearing leather and that loose clothing the gang members wear so he didn't die right away. I had to watch it happen with his older brother cursing and crying and swearing he'd kill me."

"That's awful."

"His brother's in jail. Donny's in his grave and I was cleared. Justified use of force. I was on leave for ten days and rode a desk another two. We use outside agencies to investigate and they took their sweet time. Just about drove me crazy."

"Were you hit?" She pointed at the scar through his eyebrow.

"This? Naw. I cracked this on a rock jumping off the canyon wall into the river when I was sixteen. We all jumped from that ledge as kids. As young men we all had to scale the canyon wall. I was the first one in my group to reach the top. Carter was second."

She drew a deep breath and said nothing, but her jaw was clamped tight.

"Thank you for telling me that."

He nodded and tried to focus on the road, which was a challenge with Sophia sitting beside him.

They left Piñon Forks and drove along the

river. Just past the casino he saw a familiar bright yellow pickup with black pin striping. He knew the truck and the driver, and knew he had warrants for skipping a tribal court appearance on a drugs and weapons charge.

He hit the lights. "Hold on."

"Wait a second. I can't pull someone over."

"Just stay in the SUV."

She didn't, of course. Just as soon as he had the vehicle pulled to the shoulder and was out of the SUV, she was out as well and she had her hand on her replacement weapon as he made his approach.

SOPHIA FOLLOWED JACK, noting that he had his hand on his weapon as he reached the driver side and ordered the driver to put both his hands out his window. He had the driver out of the vehicle in short order as she covered him and kept an eye on the passenger side door. There was no telling who was inside because of the tinted windows, which she hated. But when Jack made the collar, the passenger side door opened and a woman poked her head out.

"Back in the vehicle. Now!" Sophia ordered.

She couldn't see the woman's hands. Sophia kept her hand on her replacement weapon and felt the unfamiliar grip. The loaner pistol made her even more uncomfortable with the situation. This wasn't her personal weapon and she was not accustomed to using a .45 caliber.

Was he crazy, putting her in this position? The passenger stared at her from the open door.

Sophia repeated her order and the woman retreated but called to her associate.

"Trey, we got any female cops on the rez?"

Trey was pressed against the bed of his truck, feet spread wide and hands cuffed behind his back. Jack was efficient at least. Trey lifted his head to stare at her. Sophia watched the emotions play across his broad face. The look of disgust changed to one of interest. Finally a smile curled his lips as he looked at her as if she was the bounty.

"Well, well. What we got here?" he said.

Jack ignored him, keeping one hand on Trey's neck as he asked if his suspect had anything sharp on his person.

"No, man. No weapons, drugs. I'm clean. Why don't you introduce me to your bitch?"

"That her?" asked the woman from inside the truck.

Is that who? Sophia wondered.

"How 'bout you come over here so I can get a look at your fine ass," said Trey.

"Shut your mouth," said Sophia, releasing the grip on her weapon as Jack called for backup.

"Uppity little thing, too. Sassing me." Trey turned his head to speak to Jack. "She my woman, I'd crack her across the mouth. She never talk back again. I guarantee you that."

Jack escorted him by the collar to his SUV. "Yeah, well, good thing she's not yours."

She could already hear the siren of the second unit. With Trey in the back of Jack's SUV, Sophia kept her eye on the passenger in the vehicle as Jack went to speak with the young woman.

"You own this truck, Minnie?" he asked. He knew her, of course.

"Naw. I gave it to Trey. Early birthday present."

She gave it to that jerk? Sophia found her jaw clamped. She knew what this was because she'd seen it before. There had been older men suddenly interested in her during her seventeenth year. At first Sophia had been flattered. Her mother had been on to them, ready for them actually, and had chased them all off, even the gangbangers. Though Sophia later realized it was for her mother's own selfish reasons and not to protect her daughter's best interests. It was a minor miracle she had gotten out.

"You use up all your Big Money?" asked Jack.

Minnie raised her chin. "I got some left."

Sophia stared through the open window at the girl and realized with little imagination that this could have been her future, she could have squandered her one chance on someone like Trey.

This woman was actually little more than a girl, Sophia realized, and Minnie had used up her accumulated portion of the annual tribal revenue on this jerk.

"You should keep it. Don't spend it on some guy."

"He ain't some guy. He's my fiancé."

"Yeah, well, your intended is going to jail."

"He didn't do nothing," said Minnie without hesitation.

"And then they impound his property and sell it at police auction. In other words, you lose this truck."

That got her attention. She stepped out of the vehicle and Sophia plainly saw the gun in the woman's hand. Sophia had hers out and aimed. Minnie kept her weapon at her side.

"Put down the gun, now," barked Sophia. She was already in a cold sweat just thinking about shooting someone else.

The siren grew so loud that Sophia couldn't hear what Minnie replied. But she did see her drop the pistol into the sand that lined the shoulder of the road.

Tires crunched behind her and car doors slammed. Jack shouted something and Sophia kept her attention and her aim on Minnie. A uniformed tribal police officer rushed past her and ordered Minnie to place her hands on the roof of the truck. Sophia waited until the woman was in cuffs before holstering her weapon.

At Jack's direction, the officer came back with an evidence bag and gathered Minnie's gun. Then both Trey and Minnie were transferred to the marked unit and read their rights. Sophia was trembling when they pulled away.

Jack came over to where she stood by his SUV and gathered her up in his arms. She let him hold her for a moment, felt the comfort of his embrace and the callused hand that stroked her neck, lifting the tiny hairs there. Then she pushed off of him.

"Are you out of your ever-loving mind?"

Chapter Eight

"He has outstanding warrants," said Jack, as if this was reason enough.

"I'm on administrative leave. You're my escort. I'm not here to help you make a collar."

"It was a good one."

"I had to draw my weapon!"

"You sure did."

She pressed her hand to her forehead and then growled at the sky. Finally she focused back on the detective, who smiled at her with a new appreciation. She ignored the tingle that smile caused and stuck with her fury.

"Now I have to report that I drew my weapon."

He seemed puzzled now. "You *have* to do that?"

"Of course I do! While they are reviewing my fatal force encounter I have to explain why I was making arrests up here on the mountain."

"It's federal land. Your jurisdiction."

"I am on administrative leave!"

"Got it. No more collars."

"Oh, for the love of…" She got back in his SUV and slammed the door. She still had her hand pressed to her forehead when he climbed in and set them in motion. Eventually she could not stand the silence.

"My cousin told me you are the only detective up here. Is that true?"

"Yeah, but not for long. One of our guys is getting his gold shield soon."

"Not the guy that took over our collar." She hadn't really gotten a look at him except to see he was Native and young.

"No. That's Jake Redhorse. He's so green he

still has that new car smell. Good kid." Jack sighed.

"Yeah?"

He stared at the road, thinking of the Redhorse boys, Ty, Kee, Jake and Colt. He feared he'd have to arrest Ty if he didn't straighten up, and Colt...

"He's got three brothers like me. Two were in the service, like me and Carter, and they both..." Jack's words trailed off.

"They both, what?" she prompted.

"Changed. Ty is raising hell and it seems self-destructive to me. Like he's punishing himself. He won't talk about the war. At least not to me."

"Keep trying," she said.

"Colt, well, that boy is just gone."

"Mentally?"

"No, he left. Ty said he's living like some Apache survivalist in a cabin up past Turquoise Ridge. Still on our rez, I'm told, but no one but Ty ever sees him."

"What did Chekov write…? Happy families are all alike, but unhappy families are unhappy in their own way." Hers certainly had been.

"Tolstoy," said Jack.

"What?"

"Tolstoy wrote something like that."

She lifted her brows at that but said nothing. Did she think he could not or did not read?

"And he was right, I think."

Approaching from below the man-made structure, they made it to the Skeleton Cliff Dam. The dam itself spanned the river from canyon wall to canyon wall in a great gray concave ellipse that vomited water back into the river through a controlled spillway gate. A narrow road ran along the top of the dam far above them.

"According to your shaman, there is a highway patrol vehicle up there, angled to block the east entrance with the help of a movable barrier."

He cast her a look of skepticism. "I could knock him clear with this vehicle, not to mention a dump truck or tractor trailer loaded with explosives."

She turned her attention back to the gray wall looming above them.

"Placement of explosives at the top would cause minimal damage. For real compromise you would need to be inside the working of the powerhouse or at the base of the dam."

"I've been up here in our police boat."

"Is that the little fishing boat tied up near the station?"

"Yeah. I took it up here more than once on search-and-rescue, right to the foot of the dam."

"Well, do you think the words *Tribal Police* on the side improved your access?"

"Heck, anyone who can untie a knot could take that boat. Keys are in the ignition."

"Maybe you should reconsider that policy. And that little boat couldn't carry enough to do any real damage. A bigger boat would bottom out."

"That twenty-four-footer has a gross-load capacity of over fifteen hundred pounds. That's a lot of RDX," he said, mentioning the explosive he'd used in Iraq.

"They'd see it. The explosives."

"Who? There's no one up here but the guys working the dam. I could fill the livewell with explosives and they'd never see them," he said.

"The what?"

"The livewell. On our police boat. It's an insulated fiberglass container built into the hull. A livewell is used to keep fish alive after hooking them. It's watertight and locks, so we store our rifles in there."

She shook her head, dismissing this option.

"You haven't seen the size of that livewell. I can get four twenty-pound bags of ice in there and have room to spare."

"Something the size of a car trunk might do superficial damage to the base. I doubt it would crack the structure. Plus, foam is a bad choice to hold the load because it's a shock absorber. No projectiles."

He continued to the smaller utility road leading to the powerhouse. "Good to know."

There was no more than a metal gate across the road with a simple keypad for admission. He did not press the call button, but used the key code. The gate rolled back.

"They haven't changed it in a while," he said in reply to her silent question. "Carter's wife has two sisters. One of her kids went on a field trip. The gate was open in preparation for the bus."

Sophia shifted in her seat. "I see your reason for concern."

"This is only the second dam. We know it is smaller and less vital than the one at Goodwin Lake."

"Alchesay," she offered.

"Yes, but Two Mountains Lake above this

dam is still more than big enough to decimate our reservation."

"It would look like the Johnstown Flood," she said. "Let me have a look inside."

Jack drove through the gate. They did encounter a locked door at the powerhouse and a keypad. Jack tried the same code as the gate and came up empty so he used the call box.

They were buzzed in.

She pointed at the camera over the door. "They can see your uniform and you are expected."

He hoped his expression showed how not reassured he was by her observation. Inside the powerhouse they were toured around. Sophia asked questions about the capacity of the various pressurized gases that he didn't really understand. He did understand that the giant white cylinder held something explosive from the amount of time she spent on it. Their guide was very free with information and offered to have them rappel down from the top to the bottom of the dam.

"Is that access road the only way to reach the bottom?" asked Sophia.

"Unless you can swim, but I wouldn't rec-ommend that," joked their guide.

"Boat?" said Jack.

"Not permitted past the signage, ropes and floats."

Jack looked at Sophia. "Ropes and floats. Can't think how a person could circumvent protection like that."

Sophia held her tight smile but she also seemed less than reassured. The slam dunk she had hoped for had trickled away. He thought she saw the reason for their continued worry. Whether she would admit it was something else.

She waited until they were outside to address his concerns.

"Yes, I see some issues that need addressing

and we will deal with them. But BEAR has been disbanded. They are a nonentity."

"Not according to our shaman."

"Who is a member of BEAR."

"He was."

"And also an FBI informant."

"He believes in protecting the environment."

"Through terrorism."

"Without him you'd never have discovered Lupe Wrangler headed the organization."

"That's not been proved."

Sophia knew from briefings that the Pine View Wildfire had been caused by an explosion that took down the iconic private residence that broke the ridgeline. The eco-extremist group BEAR claimed credit for the disaster sending a message to others not to build in the pristine area. Whether BEAR intended the resulting devastating wildfire touched off by the blast was unclear. The FBI had determined via exhaustive investigation that Meadow Wrangler's father, Theron, headed BEAR. But she knew that Jack and his warrior society believed that Theron Wrangler was merely a figurehead and that it was her mother, Lupe, who ran the organization. Meadow's statement regarding her father's death had been considered and dismissed. There was no evidence her father had been murdered by her mother. And Meadow's statement was self-serving as she was implicated in helping her father set the fire.

"Kenshaw says that the death of Theron and the exit of his wife serve as a signal for sleeper cells to activate," said Jack.

"I've heard that." She didn't sound as if she believed it.

"We told the FBI this."

"You very well may have. But I'm an explosives expert here to consult on your concerns. I don't work on domestic terrorism except in how it relates to explosions."

"They stole a heck of a lot of explosives."

"Yes, we are aware."

"Still missing."

"Also aware. Generally, I come in after the boom."

"Well, we are trying to avoid that."

"Understood. But let me remind you, this is an unofficial visit. I do not represent the Bureau. I'm doing my cousin a favor. Now you have pointed out some weaknesses, and I can have our people contact highway patrol to shore up these holes in security. But that's all I can do."

"What about BEAR and the sleeper cells?"

"I'll share your concerns, but I am not abreast of the BEAR investigation except to say there has been progress and arrests have been made."

Jack's phone vibrated in his pocket, making him jump. He drew it out and glanced at the screen. It was Chief Tinnin.

"Hi, Chief."

"We've finished processing Trey Fields," said Wallace.

"Okay," said Jack as he waited for the other shoe to drop. His chief would not call about such a routine matter.

"He made his phone call to an unlisted number," said Wallace. "We think he mentioned Sophia."

Jack plugged his opposite ear with his finger and leaned forward to listen as his stomach roiled. "What did he say?"

"'We saw her. She's here with Detective Jack Bear Den. Right here on our rez.'"

Jack scowled as he tried to think of someone else that Trey might have been referencing and came up empty. Not good. Having a gang member use his one call to report the position of an FBI field agent was bad. Really bad.

And it was his fault. He'd forgotten his duty to protect Sophia the moment he spotted that truck like a poorly trained hound scenting a rabbit.

"We need to find out who he called."

"Working on it now."

He turned to Sophia, raising the phone so he was not speaking into the receiver. "That fatal force encounter with Nequam, did the suspected carjacker have gang ties?"

Her lovely brown eyes widened. "I don't know that."

"How was he dressed?"

"Loose clothing. Flat-brimmed ball cap."

"Yellow?"

She closed her eyes and blew out a breath, as if thinking back to the incident. Her eyes opened wide, meeting his, and she nodded.

"Yes."

"Latin Kings," said Jack.

"Yellow and black," she said, repeating what he had told her earlier in the day.

"You know how they get in, right?" he asked.

She nodded. "Women by sex. Men by crimes."

"They have to kill someone."

She nodded.

"I think you were targeted. That's why there happened to be someone right there filming."

"Because I'm FBI?"

"I doubt they knew that. Maybe just because of your black Beamer. Flash car like that makes a great target."

"I told the SAC that the witness may have been there to film the heist as evidence of the crime," she said.

"Returning with the car would do that. What they were filming was evidence of murder."

She gave an almost imperceptible shiver and folded her arms around her middle.

"We have a problem."

Jack gave her the details.

"I have to call in and report this," she said.

"They're going to pull you out of here."

"I sure hope so."

THEY CANCELED THE second visit to the second power station and headed back toward the compound. Jack called for an escort but they were still alone as they crossed into and out of the adjoining town of Darabee.

They'd had some trouble with crooked cops here so he had not called to them for assistance. It was the Darabee PD that set up the opportunity for the hit on the Lilac shooter and the nest of corruption was still being sorted out.

Sophia had been in contact with her office supervisor. As she expected, the shooting had set off alarm bells and they wanted her home. Her people were making arrangements.

She had other information. Her field office was on high alert after some intel on a possible terrorist threat to the federal offices in Phoenix. Something was happening, but they didn't have the important information, like where or when. They did know who. BEAR had sent a message by US mail warning of an impending attack.

"They've got their hands full," said Sophia.

"I may need to sit tight until they can get to me."

"We'll take you to the compound. There is one road in and we can protect that."

"There is the river," she reminded him.

He nodded. "Tribal headquarters, then. The station is a defensible position. Plus, I can get us information on Martin Nequam. Seems like this all points back to him."

"Sounds good."

Somewhere between the phone call and this moment, he and Sophia had ceased pulling in opposite directions and become a team. His police force was small, and he'd never had a partner. But havihg Sophia beside him felt like a partnership and he liked it.

Jack never saw it coming. One moment he was discussing strategy and the next he was showered with cubes of glass as the front windshield exploded.

Chapter Nine

Sophia spit out a piece of glass and ducked. She had her pistol drawn and her seat belt released just before Jack reached across the seat and shoved her to the floor of the SUV.

"Stay down," Jack ordered.

That was no rock hitting the windshield. It was a bullet, and he was darn sure they weren't shooting at him. But taking him out would make it easier to get to Sophia. And they were not getting to Sophia.

Not today. Not ever.

"What's happening?" she yelled as dust billowed in through the empty space before him.

"Someone's shooting at us."

"Location?" she asked, spinning so she could crouch down with both elbows on the seat and her pistol pointed at the ceiling.

He marveled at her dexterity. He could not even fit in that tight space, let alone maneuver in it.

"Unknown. Forward, possibly in the rocks to my left."

Another bullet struck behind him on the passenger side. He glanced back and saw daylight through the hole. Large caliber, he thought.

"Rear position," he said and accelerated. They had to be on the ridge, across the river. Using a scope. He lifted the radio and called it in.

He left the road, choosing the cover of the pines. Within a few moments he reached the narrow gap cut through the rock for the road. This position gave no shot from across the river, but if there were someone on the rock above them he had drawn them into a shooting gallery.

He braced for more gunfire.

Sophia glanced from one side of the shorn rock to the other.

"Bad spot," she said.

"But out of range."

"They could be up top." Her words mirrored his thoughts.

"If I leave this gap they have another shot at us from across the river."

"Hold then," she said, pistol raised and ready.

The radio barked as Wallace Tinnin called for a status update. Jack lifted the radio and responded. Tinnin was sending his only available men, three units, to them. Jack lifted his cell phone and called Ray Strong, told him the situation. He sent Ray and Dylan to check the opposite ridge.

"We're en route," said Ray. "You sit tight."

"Will do."

"Oh, and your mom called," said Ray.

"What's wrong?" asked Jack.

"Don't know. Call her when you can. Gotta go. We're rolling."

"Let me know what's happening when…" He glanced at the phone and saw that Ray had disconnected.

"Now what?" asked Sophia.

"We wait." Jack wondered if there were more of them. If they had forced him onto this road cut and were now approaching their position.

Sophia rose, sending the cubes of broken glass showering to the floor mats. She ran a finger into her mouth and along her cheek and dropped a bloody cube of glass to the floor with the rest.

"You all right?" Jack asked.

She didn't look at him when she nodded. All business, as she scanned for any approaching threat. From far off came the welcome sound of sirens. His department was on the way.

"That's a good sign," said Sophia.

A few minutes later Jack and Sophia contin-ued to the station under police escort.

They reached tribal headquarters, where Chief Tinnin waited, greeting them with a Kevlar vest in hand. Jack exited the SUV and took the vest, then gave it to Sophia. She needed no instructions but slipped into the oversized gear with fluid grace. The second the last strap was secure, he had her out and running for the doors, his arm around her waist and her body tucked close to him. They ran with matched strides, like a thoroughbred teamed with a draft horse.

Jack wouldn't feel safe until he had Sophia through the station doors.

SOPHIA PANTED, WITH hands on knees, the diz-ziness a result of the aftermath of her fright. Studying the effects of adrenal reaction in the academy was far different than experiencing it, and she did not object when Jack sat her in a chair and offered her a bottle of water.

She'd been prepared when she needed to be. It was all right to let her body recover now. Still it bothered her that Jack's hand was steady as he handed her the cool plastic bottle.

"This is my fault," he said.

His supervisor nodded. "It is. She's a guest. You're her escort. You don't pull over a suspect when you have a passenger."

"They might have been shooting at Detective Bear Den," said Sophia.

"Maybe," said Tinnin to Sophia, hands on his hips as he regarded them. "But it's your side of the window that's missing."

Sophia's ears buzzed and her dry throat made her cough. She sipped the water and said nothing further. Jack did not leave her side. He stayed squatting on his heels, his head nearly eye-level with hers until she finished shaking. He also held her hand. Was this just an act of comfort or did he also feel the connection between them strengthening?

"I'm all right, Jack," she said and gave him a smile.

"Still pale," he observed.

She pulled her hand back. He wasn't her sweetheart or her mother. She could deal with this like she did everything else—on her own.

"Can I get you anything? You hungry?"

She shook her head. The idea of food made her stomach clench. A glance at the station's ancient analog wall clock told her it was nearly two in the afternoon. A man Jack's size must be starving by now. She took pity on him.

"Could you order something in?"

His smile made her heart flutter. Based on the heat flooding over her skin, she'd guess the color was also returning to her cheeks.

"Fine. Turkey, ham or roast beef?" he asked.

"Roast beef with lettuce, mayo and tomato, if they have it. No onions."

He moved to the phone and placed an order with someone named Willy, adding drinks, chips and brownies.

"Want to look up Martin Nequam while we wait?" she asked.

"You recover fast," said Jack. But he sat at his desk and tapped at a keyboard so old the space bar had a shiny spot exactly where his thumb touched.

She cast a dubious glance at the cathode monitor. But soon after he'd logged in and up popped the image of a young woman.

"Who's that?" she asked.

"Missing person," said Jack. "Her name is Kacy Doka. She disappeared in February. Teens run away but she's the third since November."

"That's a lot on such a small reservation."

"I agree."

"Home troubles?"

"Don't know. Wallace just pulled me in. I've only started investigations on them collectively. Up until now they've been treated as separate cases. We want to be sure their disappearances are unrelated."

He closed the window and the bright smiling face of Kacy Doka disappeared.

Jack was searching on the Crime Information Center database. It wasn't as sophisticated as the tools available to the FBI, but would do in a pinch.

It did not take long for him to get hits on Martin Nequam.

"All right," said Jack, leaning forward.

The criminal history page popped up and displayed Nequam's date of birth. The age of the youth hit her hard, and she was glad she was still seated beside Jack's desk. A lump rose in her throat and she swallowed several times to choke it back down.

Nequam had three entries under names used. Below that came known associates, his arrest record, including the agency making the arrest, and the charge.

"Juaquin Nequam, twenty-three. Martin have an older brother?"

She shook her head. "I don't know."

Jack used the computer to look up Juaquin's information. Then he lifted the phone and called the state highway patrol, relaying the information on the shooting and the make, model and plate of his suspect. Then he repeated the call to the Flagstaff PD, asking them to check the location for Juaquin Nequam.

Jack flicked his attention back to the screen and read aloud from Martin Nequam's criminal history. "'Fleeing, convicted,'" said Jack, reading the list. "'Robbery, convicted.' Another robbery and conviction, battery and substance-abuse charge. Looks like he had some charges pending." He turned to her. "Your boy was bad news."

She couldn't meet his gaze.

"Sophia?" He reached out to her, his big hand falling over her tightly laced ones. "It's okay. It will be okay."

The warmth and the way he leaned in as he dropped his voice was her undoing. She let out a stuttering sob and pulled her hands from beneath his in order to cover her face. Tears spilled and the sobs got worse. Right here on the squad floor, she realized, she was going to release those tears she had kept inside since that night.

Jack rolled his chair to her so his legs straddled hers and he drew her forward. She nestled against his chest, clutching the soft fabric of his button-up shirt and holding it before her. His hands rubbed up and down her back. The man was really good at this. Was that why she'd finally let go—because she knew he'd be there to catch her?

"I'm s-sorry," she stammered. Her fingers were wet and his shirt damp.

"Don't be. You're under a lot of pressure. Best to let it out."

She released him to wipe her eyes and his hands continued to rub in long strokes down her back. She turned her head so that her cheek pressed to his chest. He lowered his chin, cradling her.

"I got you, Sophia. You're not alone."

She managed a nod and another sniff escaped her, but the sobs had ceased, rubbed away by his strong, gentle hands.

Sophia straightened and he rolled back in his chair, reestablishing their personal space and leaving her with a disturbing desire not to let him go. Silly. He was comforting her. Anyone would do the same. But anyone would not have left her feeling breathless and dizzy with an entirely new kind of unwelcome emotion. She wasn't sorry she kissed him last night except that now that she had done so, she wanted to kiss him again.

"You all right?" he asked, his gaze now cautious.

Oh, yeah, he could read her. She met his inquiring gaze and his brows lifted as he sat back.

"Well, here we are again," he said. "Just like last night."

"Except we are in your squad room."

"True."

"And my office is sending transport. I'm leaving tomorrow at oh-eight-hundred."

"That just adds a time clock."

"No, it makes it impossible. I don't play where I work."

"A consult. You don't work here," he reminded her. "We aren't colleagues."

"What are we then?"

"Real question is what could we be. I'd like to find out."

She glanced around and found the small room blissfully empty and the chief's office door closed. One of the advantages of a small squad room.

"I forgot to tell them I drew my weapon." She pressed a hand to her forehead.

"You okay?" asked Jack. "You're going pale again."

"I forgot to tell my supervisor I assisted in making an arrest and that I drew my weapon."

He sat back, testing the mechanics of the chair, which creaked in protest.

"Really? That's your big worry?"

"I'm on…"

"Administrative leave," he said, finishing her sentence "Yeah. Got it. But someone tried to kill you. That's not your top priority?"

That *was* messed up, she realized.

"Yeah. I know." But they could have been shooting at Jack and either way, they had missed and that was not going to go on the report that would be considered in the ongoing investigation.

"Excuse me." She lifted her phone and found the battery in the red because she hadn't charged it.

"You can use mine. I have to talk to Tinnin."

He left her and she made the call to Captain Larry Burton.

"Are you in a secure location?" asked her captain.

"Yes."

"Okay. Great."

The conversation did not go well from there, but the gist of it was that she was not to be consulting while on leave. Favor to a friend or not, her opinion as a federal officer entangled the Bureau.

When she told him about the gaps in the security at the power station, he told her he'd handle it, have the state highway patrol increase their presence.

Burton tried to get her off the phone before she managed to tell him about the shooting, but she got it in. She had his full attention, judging from the silence on the other end of the call.

She told him about the collar and her role in covering the passenger and that the suspect seemed to have mentioned her to someone during his one phone call.

Then she made a mistake, telling her captain that Martin Nequam had gang ties.

"And how do you know that?" asked her captain.

Sophia stopped talking.

"You were warned not to do any background on the deceased."

"Technically, I didn't do it."

"You're blowing it, Rivas. You know that your fishing trip could influence the outcome of your investigation. I thought getting away for a few days would be good for you."

"Captain—"

"Stop. Just stop. Your little side gig or whatever this was, it's over. I'm pulling the plug. You stay put and out of trouble until we get you home in the morning."

"Yes, sir."

"I'll be in touch." He hung up before she could give him the number at the station.

Jack emerged from the chief's office, rubbing his neck and looking equally glum.

"We're taking you to the compound."

"There's no phone service out there."

"I have a radio."

"I need to charge my phone."

"You have a charger?" he asked.

"In my car." Which was back at the compound. "Fine. Let's go."

They reached the parking lot when the food delivery arrived. Jack would not let her pay for her lunch. They took the food along in his unmarked, white F-150 pickup and were followed by Chief Tinnin. They had no further trouble en route.

Kenshaw Little Falcon greeted them at the compound, walking out to stand beside the truck and speaking to Jack the instant he opened the door.

"First I must deliver a message from your mother," said Kenshaw.

"What's wrong?"

This was the second message from his mother, and she believed that he had not returned her call.

"She said that she is coming here to see you.

She can tell you why when she arrives, but you should stay until she speaks to you."

"I have to help with the investigation. The shooting. And she shouldn't come here. It could be dangerous."

"Too late. She's coming and she doesn't carry a phone. So just stay awhile. Ray and Dylan called me. They found the shooter's position and shell casings. He was driving a pickup, which tells us very little."

Sophia slid down from the high bucket seat to the grass.

Jack grabbed their lunch from behind his seat and then walked with Little Falcon toward the lodge. She followed, glancing toward her car and wishing she could get her phone charged, but not wanting to miss what else Kenshaw might say.

Jack passed Sophia her lunch and then filled in his shaman on their two encounters and turned it over to her for a recap of the visit to the dam and power station. She shared her observations and did not hold back any of her concerns as Jack munched his sandwich. She'd be gone tomorrow morning and this tribe needed all the information they could get. Some small part of her wished she could stay, not just because Jack Bear Den made her entire body flash on and off like a Christmas light, but because she was coming to agree that they had reason for concern.

She took the seat on the porch beside Kenshaw, who faced the river. Jack preferred to lean against the porch rail in front of her, causing a visceral distraction that interfered with her ability to think and speak. The man was one giant temptation.

Perhaps her imminent departure was a blessing. One more night with him in the adjoining cabin was going to be tough. Well, it was out of her hands. Her field office was yanking her out of here and she'd be lucky not to receive a reprimand.

No good deed goes unpunished, she thought, and snorted at the truth of that.

Kenshaw listened as she finished up her description of the security concerns and fell silent.

"I do not know what you have been told about me," said the shaman. "But I would tell you some things that I do not think are in my files."

She'd read those files, of course, at least all that she'd had access to.

"I worked with a man named Cheney for a long time, since we were young men."

Her mind provided intel on Cheney. Cheney Williams, deceased. Killed in the explosion that triggered the ridge fire. Known member of BEAR and Theron Wrangler's second in command. Death ruled accidental.

"He was my friend and my contact in BEAR, but not my only one. That is why I am so concerned. My cell has been activated with the others, but I only know the target of my cell. Still, I was aware of various potential targets."

"Did you share this with my department?"

"The one in Phoenix. I worked as an informant with that field office. And I will tell you what I told them. Each cell will attack their target as soon as feasible after the death or departure of Lupe Wrangler. She has left the country. That is the signal."

"And you believe the reservoirs are a potential target."

"I know it. But since it is not the target of my cell, I do not know how or when."

"Isn't the purpose of a cell to keep their mission secret from the others?"

"It is to insulate itself and work independently. But Cheney Williams knew each cell's mission. He was to pass that information to Dylan, but Cheney was killed on the ridge in an explosion. You know where those explosives came from?"

She did. The theft at the Lilac copper mine.

"What is the target of your cell?" she asked, not really expecting an answer.

"Pipelines in Phoenix."

She sat up straight. "Does my office know that?"

"Of course. But not where and when. I have not been activated and so I have no more information."

He turned to her and held her gaze with eyes that reflected great sadness. "We were trying to save the earth. When the organization became radicalized, I had my doubts and reached out to the FBI. I hoped they could stop BEAR."

"I'm sure they will." She needed to get to a phone.

"I do not share your confidence. A small dedicated group prepared to die can accomplish great and terrible things."

That, she knew, was true.

"Which is why we need you to protect us and help us set those charges on our canyon as a fail-safe in the event BEAR succeeds in destroying that dam."

"I can't do that."

"You are our last hope."

Chapter Ten

"I can't blow up a public waterway, no matter what the reason." Sophia gripped the arms of the pine rocker angled beside a similar one holding the tribe's shaman. "You asked me here to give an opinion. Your best course is to have your leadership voice their concerns to state and federal authorities."

Jack chuckled and she glanced at him. He stood casually, leaning against the porch rail with his thumbs hitched on either side of his belt buckle.

"That hasn't gone so well in the past, historically, I mean."

The number of egregious breaks in federal

contracts to Native people was a debate for another time. She wasn't here to defend the US government. But she was trying to be part of the change she wanted in the world.

"I can't do it," she said.

"We understand. And we are sorry for the trouble you have had here," said Kenshaw. "I am embarrassed and concerned that a guest would be attacked on our land."

"Thank you."

Kenshaw gazed toward the gently flowing river, which was carefully controlled by the outlet of the powerhouse and dam just northeast of their land. She watched the water, trying not to think of the millions of gallons contained by concrete and steel. What would happen to his people if the dam was destroyed.

"Perhaps moving your population would not be a bad idea," she said. "Just temporarily."

Jack's radio crackled and the police officer stationed at the top of the road reported the arrival of Jack's family.

"Family?" he asked, straightening.

Kenshaw turned to Sophia. "Jack has his parents and three brothers. Kurt works in Darabee. Thomas is with ICE on the border, a Shadow Wolf hunting drug traffickers. And Jack's twin, the oldest, Carter, is with his wife."

"With the Department of Justice." She knew that, of course, and knew that the trial for the men who had tried to kill his wife was now underway.

Jack was already off the porch and standing by the twin ruts that served as a road.

"We believed Carter and his wife, Amber, would need relocation. But the man she was testifying against is dead."

"I understood the trial was moving forward."

"Not those men. I mean Theron Wrangler."

Now *that* she did not know and she was instantly curious as to what information these witnesses might have.

Kenshaw watched her with intent eyes and a knowing smile.

"Amber Bear Den, Carter's wife, is the only link between the Lilac mine massacre and Theron Wrangler. It was why BEAR tried so hard to kill her."

"And she's no longer in danger?"

"The information is useless now. She has nothing on Lupe, Theron's wife."

She'd heard the theories that Lupe ran BEAR. It was her department's belief that Theron was the leader and not a front. But now she began to wonder.

"She was careful," said Kenshaw. "I will give Lupe that."

Sophia could hear the roar of a truck engine now and the creaking of old struts. Jack lifted his gaze toward the vehicle she could not see.

"Carter has a wife and Jack has been missing his brother. Jack has friends and Kurt, but he has still seemed to be very lonely, to me."

"Jack, he's not…attached?"

Kenshaw smiled as he continued to watch the river and she continued to wish she could go back in time and not ask her last question.

"Jack feels unattached. His appearance has been a great burden to him."

"Because he's so big?" She liked that.

"Because he is so different. Anyone with eyes can see, but it is always his women who ask. They make him face what he would ignore. He cannot stand that and so he is alone."

Note to self, she thought—*don't ask him why he looks different than his brothers.*

"Well, that's too bad," she said.

"Yes. But he needs to face his differences to accept himself as we have all accepted him."

Get him to accept himself but don't mention the differences. Check. How did she do that?

"Could I borrow your phone?" she asked.

Kenshaw passed her a small black older-model phone. She called her department in Flagstaff and relayed what Kenshaw had told her about the pipeline. They took down the information. Then she called Luke to be sure his field office was aware. They were.

"And I don't appreciate that you ditched me up here," she said.

"Mountain air will help you sleep and having problems bigger than your own is good for you," said her cousin.

"They sure are bigger."

"Call if you need me," said Luke and the line went dead.

A problem bigger than herself. Sophia's gaze lifted to the road and landed on Jack Bear Den.

JACK STOOD IN the road, facing the approaching vehicle. He couldn't see it yet. But he could hear it, caught the sound of an engine and a radio playing classic rock.

A familiar truck rolled into view. He knew his father's vehicle on sight. The older model Ram had four doors and both front and rear seats. Judging from the sag in the suspension, that rear seat was full. Jack recognized his father, Delane, driving and his mother, Annetta, in the passenger seat. Between them he could see Kurt. But as they drew closer he realized that he was not looking at the face of his youngest sibling, but the thin face of Carter.

Jack broke into a run, charging the truck like a bull. His father hit the brakes and his mother managed to slide out of the seat before Jack reached into the truck and hauled Carter Bear Den to him and squeezed.

"They didn't tell me!" he said, hugging his twin and feeling the changes. Carter had lost weight.

"Easy, bro. You're crushing me."

Jack eased his grip and drew back to stare at the familiar face he had so missed.

"You back?" he asked.

Carter nodded and wiped the tears from his cheeks. Jack swallowed at the lump in his throat.

"I missed you, brother," said Carter.

Jack glanced away to keep from blubbering and met his mother's tear-streaked face. It was his undoing. He couldn't seem to get enough air.

"We wanted to surprise you," she said, her voice quavering like a bird's. "They just got back."

From the smaller rear door emerged Amber and Kurt. Amber stepped forward and he gave her a kiss, careful not to crush her as he had his brother. She also looked drawn, with circles under her eyes. The ordeal of witness protection and the trial had taken an obvious toll.

Kurt slapped Jack on the shoulder. "Surprised?"

Jack grinned and glanced back at the porch, where both Kenshaw and Sophia watched the reunion. Kenshaw knew, of course. But Sophia did not. She beamed at him, clearly pleased at his joy and his heart squeezed a little tighter.

He motioned her to join them. Her smile vanished and she shook her head. He motioned again. She set her jaw, but descended from the porch.

Jack made introductions and Carter and Amber politely shook her hand, but it was clear they had both had enough of FBI and DOJ officers. Kenshaw called them all into the lodge.

"Casseroles," he said. "I sent out a call and have them in the oven."

They all gathered in the lodge at the circular table and Jack was astonished at how much Carter and Amber ate.

"Didn't they feed you out there?" asked his mother.

Out there. It was how the people referred to anywhere that was not right here, on their land.

Sophia sat between his father and Kenshaw and seemed to Jack to be trying to disappear. He did not have to be the most perceptive of men to realize she was genuinely uncomfortable surrounded by his family.

Tommy arrived in time for dessert, adding to the gaiety and the volume of conversation as they each talked over each other in a rush to catch up on the missing months.

In the evening they lit a fire outside and brought out the large drum. Kenshaw and his father set the rhythm, with all three of this brothers and him keeping pace. Jack thought they'd never sounded so good as they sang. Sparks from the fire rose into the clear dry air and lifted skyward to the glittering stars.

Amber and his mother and Sophia clapped to the rhythm. They broke their song only to greet Ray, Morgan and Lisa, who'd arrived. Amber noticed immediately that Morgan was expecting and offered congratulations. The two old friends linked arms and were just heading toward the drum circle when Dylan and Meadow arrived.

Then the circle formed again and Jack thought of his medicine wheel talisman and the circle of friends and family that formed this living sacred hoop.

The men drummed and the women sang, Meadow keeping the general melody, though not knowing the language, her attempts to sing made everyone laugh. The party broke up very late. Carter and Jack walked toward the river. Jack knew in his head he would see Carter in the morning, but it was hard to let go after missing him for so long and so very much.

"It's been tough without you here, brother."

"I missed the ridge fire," said Carter. "Heard Ray stepped in. Always figured it would be Dylan as captain."

He was talking about the historic Pine View wildfire. Of course, as a Hotshot, it would have killed Carter not to be able to deploy with his crew. The Turquoise Canyon Hotshots were among the most elite crews in the country.

"He couldn't. Dylan was caught in it with Meadow. Had to deploy his fire shelter over both of them."

Carter's eyes widened. "No."

"He can tell you all about it. Love to, I'm sure."

"I've got a lot of catching up to do," said his brother.

Jack tried to imagine missing all that had happened since his brother had followed his wife into witness protection in February. Eight months.

"How did things go with the test results? Did you get your answers?"

Jack looked away.

"Jack?"

"Never opened them," he admitted. Though he'd carried them in his wallet every day since they'd arrived in March.

Carter placed a hand on his shoulder. "Want me to do it?"

"No." He faced his twin. "I'll do it. Now that you're home. I will."

Headlights rolled across them as his father pulled the truck around.

Carter stared back across the darkness, hearing Ray and Dylan bid each other good-night as they made for their cabins with Amber and Meadow.

"You want me to stay? Help keep an eye on Sophia?"

Jack took one look at his brother and made the call. "We got it. You go home with your wife."

"She's pretty," said Carter.

"Who?"

"Don't give me that. You couldn't take your eyes off her when she was singing."

"That's because she doesn't speak our language."

"Western Apache. Yeah. They're different. Not as different as Dylan and Meadow. Boy is that a mismatch. Can't even believe Dylan is going to marry her. He's always been so traditional."

"The heart leads where it leads," said Jack, quoting their mother.

"Right. Well, good night."

"'Night. Glad to have you back, brother."

"Likewise."

Jack watched him walk away, knowing his mother would be making fry bread in the morning and Carter would begin gaining back the weight he had lost. Still smiling, he wandered back to the porch to wave his family off.

Kenshaw turned in, leaving Sophia and Jack standing alone by the road.

"You have a lovely family," said Sophia. Her voice held an undertone of something, a kind of stiffness that resonated inside him. What was wrong?

"Yeah. You know, my mom looks so happy. She'll probably put this in the classifieds, too."

"The classifieds?"

"Yeah. It's silly, but she makes announcements there. Stuff like 'Carter and Jack are back from overseas. Welcome home, boys!' She always posts one for birthdays and when something big happens."

"Might not be a great idea to say her eldest son is back from witness protection," said Sophia.

"You got that right.

"Do you have siblings?" asked Jack.

"Yes, lots. But we weren't raised together."

His brows lifted, and he wished that just once he had not been right.

"No?" he said, half hoping she'd keep her problems to herself, the other half recognizing that she was about to share something personal.

"Fostered. All of us. I was number eight. They broke us up when my father went to prison. It's a common story."

All too common.

"Mom?"

"She's around. Can't really take care of herself, let alone her kids. Doesn't stop her from having them, though. I stayed with my granny until she passed. She raised me."

"That's tough, Sophia." And made her current position with the FBI even more impressive. The odds had definitely been stacked against her.

"All I ever wanted was to get off the rez. When I was a kid I wanted clean clothes. Once I got to foster care, I wanted a room that was mine."

"And you have that now."

She nodded, meeting his gaze with sad eyes. Was she thinking of losing all she had gained? She would if she did as his tribe wished. How could he ask her to risk losing everything she had achieved? Jack glanced over his shoulder to the river and knew the answer. If they didn't do something, all he knew would be washed away.

"Let me walk you back to your cabin."

They strolled across the grass, neither in any hurry to arrive.

"I'm sorry to put you in this position, Sophia."

She shook her head. "Don't be. I've given

you my suggestions. Tomorrow my escort will be here and I'll be back home. But, Jack, you should move your people. Send them up to my reservation. They'd take them in."

"My tribe fought long and hard to establish a reservation of our own. We are not leaving it."

They passed the fire pit as the drenched embers smoldered and smoking logs shifted. The members of the Turquoise Canyon Hotshots knew better than to leave a fire unattended and had carefully doused the flames and scattered the fuel inside the stone fire pit.

Sophia and Jack continued on, pausing on the porch of her cabin.

It was their last night together. Jack gazed down at Sophia.

"They're coming for you in a few hours," he said, the clock ticking louder now.

"Oh-eight-hundred hours, yes. I won't have time to check the uppermost dam."

"Sophia, I'd like to kiss you again." He'd like to do more than kiss her if she'd let him.

He wanted to know her as a man knows a woman and keep some part of her here in his heart.

"Will you come in?" she asked, opening the door.

Chapter Eleven

"I'd like that very much," said Jack in answer to Sophia's invitation.

She moved aside and Jack stepped past her into the darkness. His eyes adjusted slowly, the light from the windows casting blue starlight across the floor. Each cabin was identical within, with a table and chairs, sitting chair and a full-size bed centered on the back wall next to a bedside table. He waited for her to close the door and throw the latch, then gathered her in his arms.

He leaned in to inhale the sweetness of her neck, but she drew back, making him pause.

"You understand that I'm leaving tomorrow?" she asked.

"Yes."

"This won't change anything."

It would change everything, he knew. But he murmured, "Yes," as his lips brushed her neck.

She trembled as he trailed kisses down the column of her throat and into the vee left by her prim, professional blouse. She worked the buttons, releasing them until the garment flapped open. He breathed in her sweet scent.

"Lavender," he whispered against the swell of her breasts.

She backed away, gripping his shirt in both fists as she led him across the room to the bed. Halfway there she released him to slip out of her shoes and drop her blazer, then unfastened the clip that held her shoulder holster. She lay the weapon on the bedside table. He placed his beside it with his wallet and radio. His fingers trembled as he groped for the square packet in his wallet, causing the letter to fall to the floor. She stooped and retrieved it as he found the condom. She set the folded envelope on the table beside the weapons and shucked out of her slacks. He watched her shrug out of the blouse, which fluttered to the floor, leaving her in only her white lace bra and matching panties. Her skin glowed blue in the starlight. She was all soft curves and smooth skin. He was all coarse hair and muscle, by comparison.

He unbuttoned his shirt slowly, hoping she would not have second thoughts when she saw him shirtless. He didn't often remove his shirt because it emphasized the dissimilarity between him and other men here. His body type was so different and his chest was covered with thick curling hair. He dropped his shirt and waited.

Sophia's gaze raked over him. Finally she lifted her eyes to meet his. He did not see revulsion or fear, but hunger. He released a breath. She reached for his jeans and let her unzip them before he sat to tug off his boots and then his jeans.

She moved to stand between his legs, her thighs brushing his. Jack lifted his hands and rested them lightly at her waist.

"I'm not too big?" he asked, voicing aloud the fear he carried with him like his skin.

"Not for me." Her fingers raked down his chest, scraping through the chest hair and over his muscles. "You look more like a lumberjack than a guy riding in a police unit all day."

"Sometimes I ride a horse," he said. "A lot of our rez is easier to get to that way."

She moved closer, allowing him to brush his hands up the long muscles of her back. He lifted her and spun her to the bed, easing her down beside him. He pushed the bra up and away. She lifted to let him drag it off. She shrugged out of her panties.

Jack remained on his side, giving himself the gift of seeing her completely naked and stretched out before him wearing nothing but a seductive smile. There was something dark on her breast—a tattoo? He thought it unlikely, but the possibility made him grow even harder. Sophia was full of surprises, including giving in to the heat and hunger roaring between them, if only for one night.

God, he hadn't even had her and he wanted her again. But he waited for her to make the approach.

He looped a thumb under the tie holding her thick hair and dragged it free. Her hair fanned the pillow.

"You're beautiful," he said, his fingers trailing over her shoulder and back up to her hair.

"So are you."

She rolled to her side, facing him now, and inclined her head so that her cheek brushed the back of his hand.

"Not too big?" he asked again.

She chuckled. "I like big."

The tension crackled between them as he waited and prayed she would reach out to him, his hand trailing down her arm and back to the blanket.

Sophia moved closer, dragged a hand down his naked chest, her fingernails making his nerves blast awake. He growled in pleasure, the sound vibrating through his chest.

"I have protection." He reached back for the condom, already wishing he carried more than two.

"Me, too."

She was cautious. That was smart. Her caution was probably why she'd made it out of foster care and avoided getting pregnant as a teen. He admired her for so many reasons. But right now the aching want was descending over his brain. He needed his skin pressed to hers, to feel her breath on his neck and her nails rake over his back.

He loomed over her and she looped her arms around his neck and pulled, sending a barrage of hot kisses down his neck and chest, trailing lower until she reached his waistband.

His arms, usually so strong, began to tremble as her fingers slipped beneath his underwear. She released him, peeling back the fabric that separated them.

She tore open the condom package with her teeth, pushing him to his back. He complied, falling to the mattress and letting her slip the protective sheath over the length of him.

His stomach twitched and tightened as she kissed her way back up his body, finally finding his mouth. He cradled her head as he kissed her long and deep.

When she slipped a leg across him and straddled his hips, he watched them come together. She lowered herself and Jack closed his eyes to savor the bliss that carried them both late into the night.

They slept tangled in sheets and blankets. He felt her shivering in the heart of the night and dragged the blanket over her, tucking it up around her shoulders and then pulling her close to his chest, sharing his heat. She snuggled against him and he breathed a sigh at the perfect moment. The sense of calm and the ache of want mingled to form an unnameable desire that beat with each stroke of his heart. He closed his eyes to better sense each warm breath that flowed from her and across his chest. Jack cradled her head and kissed her forehead. Deep in sleep, Sophia muttered something that was an attempt as speech. He stroked her head, his fingers tangling in the satin of her hair, loose at last.

"Shhh," he whispered.

She relaxed back to slumber. Jack tried to stay awake a few minutes more. But the satisfaction of their joining and the lethargy that followed was too much and he tumbled to sleep, still cradling her close.

This was special, his heart murmured. She was special.

He woke when she slipped from his arms before dawn. He grasped her hand to stay her.

"Be right back," she promised and he let her go.

She would be. But Jack did not fool himself. Sophia would not stay with him for long. He'd been okay with that when she arrived. But things were changing and he wasn't sure just what to do about that.

The bathroom door opened and closed, water ran and she was there beside him again. She slipped over him, one thigh gliding across his stomach until she lay on top of him like a second skin. Her body was warm and her muscles slack. He stroked her back, gently but with purpose, to rouse her from her sleepiness. Her breathing changed first, then she started to move, climbing up until her mouth met his. Her kiss and the rocking of her hips left no doubt that she wanted him again.

This time was slow and sweet. Their pleasure vibrated like a taut cord until they broke together in a hot rush of sensation.

Would he ever get enough of his spider

woman? Not if he had a thousand years, he decided. He'd had women, but none was Sophia's equal. She was poised and strong and experienced in the ways of the world, with enough sexual confidence to keep him guessing.

She was a survivor who had beaten the odds and made something of herself with very little help. His admiration only strengthened his desire.

They dozed and when he next woke the light was pink, giving everything a rosy glow. He scowled at the window and the light that peeked through, knowing they were coming for her today and that they would take her from him.

He wondered if she would agree to see him again, or if this was, to her, just a one-time affair.

She slipped from the bed and back across the room. He could see her scoop the white bra from the ground and slip it around her torso, fasten the clasps and spin the undergarment back into place. He understood the meaning. She was back to business and preparing for the day.

Her cousin, Luke Forrest, was coming to take her back to Flagstaff under escort. It might be safer for her there, but he didn't like the idea of relinquishing custody. He knew their force was small and resources were limited. His mind knew it, but his heart wanted to be the one protecting her.

Sophia slipped into her panties.

She stood beside the bed. Jack sat up, the sheet and blankets covering him from midthigh to his waist. If she wanted modesty, he would go along. But after what they had just shared, it seemed sad.

Things were always different in daylight. He knew that.

"Good morning," he said.

She cast him a bright smile. "Yes. It is."

He did not know if she referred to the lingering satisfaction from their night together, or her anticipation at leaving. Jack did not like the uncertainty that settled in the pit of his stomach.

"I wanted to be ready when they come for me," she said.

"I understand." *Say something,* he thought. *Ask her to stay.*

Sophia leaned forward, her fingers brushed along his neck and then she lifted the cord to his medicine bundle. The small leather pouch had been beaded with a medicine wheel in white, black, red and yellow, the wheel segmented into four sections, the symbol as sacred as the cross to many in his tribe. His father said that all things of importance moved in a circle. Inside the pouch were a few blessed objects he used in ceremony and to help ground, protect and inspire him.

"Very traditional for a guy who wears his hair cut so short." She ran her hands through his hair in emphasis.

He didn't address the comment about his

short hair. If she saw his natural curls, she might understand why he preferred to keep it short, eliminating the sight of one more difference between himself and his people. He looked away and glanced at the folded envelope from Relative Finder Lab in California.

He forced his attention back to the medicine wheel, the symbol that had been chosen for him by his shaman. The hoop had special powers for healing and protection. He supposed a lawman could use all the protection he could get. But his shaman had not picked this emblem to protect, or to mark the seasons or the stages of a man's life. He had chosen it because it marked the four directions. And Kenshaw had told him the medicine wheel would help guide him.

"I have one here, too." He placed his fingers on the back of his neck. He could not see the tattoo except in his mind. "My shaman said it would help me know which way to go."

She leaned forward, her stomach pressing

momentarily to his chest. It was hard not to capture her there, her skin felt so amazing against his.

"Hmm," she said. "Did he pick the symbols for your friends, too?"

"Yes," said Jack.

"It's different than the others. Isn't it? I mean they are all medicine shields and all have five feathers. But I saw Carter's. It's a bear track on a shield. And your friend Dylan also had a track. Seemed like a puma."

"Bobcat," he said, correcting her.

"And Ray's is the head of a bald eagle, also on a shield."

Sophia drew one finger down his back, counting to five. "You each have five feathers but there are only four of you."

He wished for a moment that she was not an investigator.

"We got them after leaving the service. Kenshaw helped us pick the symbols and placement. We picked the feathers. One for each of us and the fifth feather is for Yeager Hatch. He was the friend who didn't come back."

"Bear is your family's symbol. Shouldn't you have a bear paw like your brother?"

Jack nodded. He had always thought so.

She laced her fingers behind his neck and leaned back to look at him.

"Why didn't you put it on your right arm, like the others?"

He lowered his head. He had done as his shaman had suggested, but he had wanted the tattoo on his arm.

One more way he was different. He didn't know the reason his shaman had chosen to place the medicine wheel on his back and had never found the courage to ask him.

"It doesn't show under my uniform or a short-sleeved shirt," said Jack. It wasn't the reason. He was sure there was more.

"I suppose." Sophia seemed to be humoring him. "Carter has scars all over that arm and one right through that tattoo."

"Bullet wound. He got it saving Amber," said Jack. "The other scars are older. Burns from the war."

She nodded, absorbing that admission. "Why is Dylan a bobcat?"

"Bobcats have stealth. Dylan needs that quality, needs to see what is hidden."

"Then the eagle is to give Ray perspective?" she asked.

"Yes, and to remind him that he is holy, like all things. Ray was very hard on himself about Hatch. He's better since Meadow joined him."

"What did Kenshaw say about this?" she asked, her finger circling his tattoo.

He didn't want to tell her.

"I'll show you mine," she offered as compensation.

He let his gaze rake down her perfect skin. Sophia stood before him. She reached across her body with one hand and lowered the strap of her bra, revealing her right breast beneath the white lace cup. There was a dream catcher the size of a silver dollar. Inside the web was a tiny black spider.

Jack moved to sit at the edge of the bed, so he could get a closer look.

"Spider born of butterfly," he said. He touched the mark on her perfect skin. Her nipple hardened instantly, though he had not touched it.

His body went hot and pulsed to readiness.

"Exactly. She's a hunter, like me—catching bad guys is what I do. Seemed appropriate."

"In our legends, the four spiders wove the cords that hold up the world," he said.

She turned to him. "Same with us."

They were both Apache. But the differences extended beyond their languages.

"I also have a butterfly. Want to see?" Her thumb hooked the waistband of her panties.

He did, but if it was where he thought it might be, showing him would drive him into the most obvious of actions. He wanted his brain working for a few more minutes, but not as much as he wanted to be inside her again.

He met her gaze. Her lips curled in a smile of anticipation and her attention dropped to the sheets and blankets now doing little to conceal that he was beyond ready for her.

"Well?" she asked as their gazes locked.

He nodded, hungry for her now.

She presented her back, peering over her shoulder at him. Then she lowered the lace panties to reveal a perfect monarch butterfly on the curve of her buttock.

"Butterfly born of spider," he whispered.

He reached for her and she stepped away, waving a finger at him.

"I'd love to, Jack. I mean it. But they're likely on their way. I don't want them to find me like this." She waved at her matching bra and panties.

He thought she never looked more appealing. Then his mind flashed images of their night together. He'd seen her look more appealing because last night her eyes had flared with desire for him.

"No, I understand. But maybe you'd be safer here."

"This is where they shot at me, Jack."

"I meant here at the compound." He meant here in his arms, he realized.

She made a face. Was it too much like her childhood, the rugged little cabin with no air conditioning or electricity? He liked hearing the birds and the wind, but she was a city girl now.

"You don't have enough men to guard me 24/7. The Bureau has resources."

"I'd guard you 24/7," he said.

She cast him an indulgent smile, perhaps assuming a double entendre that he had not intended.

"Would you like coffee? I'm heading to the lodge to make some."

"Yeah. Sounds good. Wait for me."

"I think I can make it." She slipped into her blouse and then shrugged into her shoulder holster, and picked up her pistol.

Jack got up and into his jeans. He'd use the lodge bathroom, he decided, because she was not walking around unescorted. He trusted Jake Redhorse, the tribal officer who covered the road overnight, but the river was still a highway and anyone with a small craft could reach them via the Hakathi River. Which reminded him, he needed to be sure they relieved Jake, who had volunteered to cover the road. The young officer was rapidly becoming Jack's go-to man for important assignments.

Jack ducked into his shirt and clipped his holster and his radio to his belt. Then he tucked the envelope back in his wallet and put them in his front pocket.

"You want to talk about that?" she asked, glancing in the direction of his wallet.

"Over coffee maybe."

She followed him out and across the wide open stretch between the row of cabins and the lodge. The scent of ash from last night's fire reached him and made him smile.

"You have a wonderful voice," she said.

"You could hear me over the others?" he asked.

"Of course. You don't sound anything like them. Your voice is much deeper."

His proud smile vanished as she pointed out just one more way he was different.

He let the conversation die as he held open the door for her. What was the use? He needed her to help the tribe. That was why she was here and that was what he should be focused on.

Chapter Twelve

Sophia headed straight for the large drip coffeemaker, filling the reserve with water and then measuring out the coffee into the filter. Then she flicked the switch and stood back to watch.

"Can't seem to get moving without a cup," she said.

Jack excused himself to wash up. When he returned, she was sitting at the counter sipping her coffee. Beside her was an empty stool and a full steaming mug.

He sat and they drank coffee side by side as they watched the river roll beyond the picture window. The familiarity struck him, and the longing. He swallowed it back with the next gulp.

"You got me dead curious about that letter. Looks like lab results. You okay, Jack?" Her dark eyes regarded him and he saw the investigator again.

"Not sick, if that's what you mean. But you are right. It's a DNA test. Carter and I sent in a swab from each of our cheeks."

She didn't ask why but cut straight to the point. "You want to know if you've got different parents."

"Parent. My mom. I think, suspect…"

"I see. Easier to sneak around behind her back than come out and ask her?"

He cradled his mug, rolling the base in a circle.

"I asked. She said she's never been with anyone but my dad."

Sophia's look told him that she didn't believe this, either.

Jack muttered a curse.

"Why haven't you opened it?"

He couldn't explain it. He just hadn't yet.

"Maybe I'm drumming up the courage."

She snorted at this. "You don't lack courage, Jack."

He didn't argue.

Sophia released her mug and spun the stool that turned in complete circles.

"But if you don't open it, you don't have to face what's inside. Me? I'd need to know."

He reached for the envelope and extracted it from his wallet. He held it between a thumb and index finger for a moment. Then he placed it on the counter and pushed it toward her.

She looked from the folded offering and then back to him, brows lifted in a silent question. He nodded.

"Okay." She straightened the envelope and ironed it once with the side of her hand. Then she unceremoniously tore open the side. Sophia upended the contents and the pages dropped out into her open hand. She spread out the pages and studied them for just a moment. Then she glanced at him, a frown on her face. It was all he could do not to snatch the letter and shove it back in the envelope. But like Pandora's box, the damage was done and at least one person knew his secret.

"What does it say?" he asked, displeased at the squeak in his voice.

"Your mother told a half truth."

"A lie."

"Misrepresentation," she amended.

Jack pressed his hands on the counter. "Sophia. You're killing me."

"Well, it says that siblings with common parents share all the same DNA, basically scrambled."

"Are you going to tell me what the results say, or not?"

"Yes, that's what I'm doing. If you have a different parent, say your father, then you'd share half the DNA as your brothers."

"Sophia, just give me the results." He extended his hand.

She drew the pages away, holding them to her chest and meeting his impatient stare with one of worry.

"Okay, fine. See?" She pointed to a table and read the first column. "Parent-child, full siblings have fifty percent shared DNA. Half siblings, your suspicion, share twenty-five. That's the same with aunts, uncles and the grandparent-grandchild relationship. First cousins share only twelve-point-five percent. Half cousins even less."

He stared at the ceiling. Then he let his head drop. Finally he met her gaze.

"What does all that mean?"

"Carter is not your brother."

Jack felt a pain in his heart as the information sliced into him like a jagged shard of glass.

SOPHIA KNEW THAT LOOK. It was the look of a man whose world was coming apart. The fabric that glued him to this place and to his family had been shredded by this information.

"Give it to me. I'll put it back." He groped for the pages, his hands trembling now. Sweat beaded on his brow.

She pressed a hand over his. "No, Jack. Just listen."

"I can't. I don't want…" He was tugging at the pages now. She lifted her hand and he made a terrible job of folding the sheets. Then he tore the envelope trying to cram the pages back inside it.

Finally he sat still, gripping the tattered envelope in two hands as if the information inside could be crushed by the pressing of his thumb and fingers.

"I knew it," he whispered. "Always."

You only had to have eyes to see he wasn't a Bear Den, she thought.

"Jack, your mother isn't your biological mother."

He looked at her, his eyes red-rimmed. His

shoulders rounded. He looked completely defeated. She felt a righteous indignation on his behalf.

"What?" His head was cocked to the side like a dog trying to understand speech and failing badly.

"They should have told you, Jack."

"So what does that mean? I'm adopted?"

"I'm not sure. But your test says that you and Carter are first cousins, so you share two common grandparents."

"Two?" He shook his head, still lost. His broad hand now rhythmically rubbed his forehead.

"If I had to guess, I'd say Annetta's parents are your grandparents. It could be your father, Delane, of course. But I don't think so. You both resemble Annetta more strongly around the eyes."

"What are you talking about?"

He'd been vested in the secret that his mother had cheated on his dad for so long. But now she was switching his secret and his mind just couldn't grasp it.

"In other words, you are the child of Annetta's brother or sister."

"She doesn't have any brothers or sisters."

Now Sophia angled her head, lifting her brows at the same time to give him a look that said *I don't think so.*

He shook his head in denial.

"I wouldn't be too sure about that."

"What are you saying, that my mother left me with my aunt and disappeared? And not one member of my tribe happened to mention it to me? That's not possible."

"When you have eliminated the impossible, whatever remains, however improbable, must be the truth."

He blasted out a breath from his nose. "You're quoting the writing of Arthur Conan Doyle now?"

"It's what happened. I don't know why she

kept it from you, why everyone here kept it from you. But in a way you are lucky."

He wouldn't look at her now. "How do you figure?"

"You have a family that loves you and something else. You have possibilities. Who and why? I'd give anything not to know who my parents are and where I come from."

She slipped from the stool and took the envelope from him, folded it and attempted to return it to his front pocket. He turned to face her, extending his leg so she could push the report away. Then he captured her around the waist and pulled her into the vee of his legs. She rested her hands on his chest and smiled at him.

"You are who you make yourself, not who you were born. Don't spend too much time back there in the past, Jack. It's not healthy."

"It doesn't matter to you?"

"Your roots? Nope. Not at all. Who I am is not where I come from or how I look. To know me you have to look much deeper than all that."

He kissed her then, his mouth hungry as his tongue slid into hers. He tasted of coffee mingled with desire. Sophia laced her fingers around his neck and leaned in.

"You two still at it?" said a male voice from the doorway.

Sophia stiffened and drew back. Jack kept the pressure on her lower back, allowing her to retreat only so far.

She turned to see Ray Strong stride into the room. His face seemed freshly scrubbed and his short hair was wet. He wore jeans, moccasins and a tight T-shirt...and a cocky smile.

"I thought you'd be worn out by now," said Ray.

Jack winced at the comment. Clearly they'd been overheard last night.

Sophia's eyes widened and she broke away from him like a bucking bronc out of the shoot. Her face went pink and her mouth dropped open.

Jack cast Ray a glare that should have dropped him in his tracks. Instead Ray held that stupid grin that had gotten him into more jams than Jack could count. Well, this time his antics had dragged in both Jack and Sophia.

"Shut up, Ray," Jack said.

Ray scratched his chest and yawned. "When you said you'd convince her to help us, well… I misunderstood. Good for you two. Morgan says you're perfect for each other."

Sophia hurried past Ray to the door.

"Sophia, wait," said Jack.

She didn't, of course.

Jack glanced back to Ray. "What is wrong with you?"

"I was congratulating you." Ray seemed oblivious to the damage he had caused.

Jack grabbed him by the T-shirt and yanked him forward. Ray lifted both hands in instant surrender.

"You made it seem that I used sex to make her help us."

"Didn't you?" asked Ray.

Now he really was going to hit him. What did Ray think Jack was, Mata Hari?

He drew back his fist.

The door crashed open. "Hey!"

Jack looked up toward the female voice. Morgan stood in the doorway and her glare was aimed at him. Jack pushed Ray away, sending Ray staggering back several steps.

"What did you do?" asked his new wife.

"Nothing. I was congratulating them."

Morgan made a sound of frustration in her throat and stared at the ceiling. Then she met Jack's gaze.

"I'm sorry, Jack."

Not as sorry as he was. He had to make Sophia understand that last night was not about getting her onboard. He cleared the door and scanned the yard. She hadn't gone far, just to the end of the porch. She stood facing the river, arms clamped across her chest.

He had covered half the distance when his radio sounded.

It was Cecil Goseyum, one of their tribal council members. Not only did Cecil do some of the best leatherwork in the tribe, but he also volunteered with the fire department. On the weekends and evenings, when Olivia was off, they covered the incoming calls to the station.

"Jack, you there?"

He lifted the radio. "Yes, Cecil. What's up?"

"I just called Wallace. He said to call you, too. I got the Phoenix news on here. There's been an explosion in the city."

Jack stopped walking.

"What kind of explosion?"

Sophia turned, her arms dropping to her sides.

"High-pressure pipelines. It's bad, Jack."

Sophia's steps were brisk. "I have to go."

He clasped her arm as she walked by him,

halting her so they stood facing in opposite directions, staring at each other.

"You're on leave."

"They'll want me back for this. I've got to go. Now."

JACK GOT HER to the police station in Piñon Forks. There Jack saw the news on the television as she tried unsuccessfully to reach her supervisor.

Someone had hit three locations in Phoenix at once. Apparently dressed as employees of the natural gas company down there, they had blocked and dug up the streets right over the major pipelines. They used backhoes and took out the major excess flow valves first, then waited for the gas to accumulate before igniting the free-flowing stream.

You didn't need to be an explosives expert to know what happened next. They had it on every downtown security camera. The workers, the breaks and the resulting fireball. Three sites. Two downtown, both banks, both among the largest buildings in the city. The third site was south, on the edge of town, an industrial complex used by a mining company as a distribution center. It was unique, Jack thought, because of its size, 250,000 square feet, and because it was owned by a company that violated the earth. Mining again. Just like the Lilac copper mine.

It was BEAR. He was sure of it.

That meant Kenshaw was right. The eco-extremist group wasn't broken. The cells were all working independently now and each had their own target. He couldn't keep himself from glancing out the window at the gently flowing river. The river where he learned to swim, canoe and fish had become an enemy.

Chapter Thirteen

This could not be happening. Sophia hunched over the phone and spoke to her captain, Larry Burton.

"But I should be there," she said, working hard to keep her voice level.

Burton's tone was rushed, as if he was on the move as he spoke. The man did not have time to chat.

"You're still on administrative leave."

"But—"

He cut her off. "I asked. It's a no. You are *not* to report."

"That can't be right."

"You need to be requested back." He spoke

slowly now, as if to be certain she heard and complied. "That's an order. Now I have to go."

She gave up on the voice-modulation thing. "I'm an explosives expert!"

"And you are not the only one in the Bureau, Rivas. We can manage without you. Okay?"

"What am I supposed to do? Sit up here twiddling my thumbs?"

"I'm sorry, Soph. Gotta go. I'll call when I can."

"Wait. Is it BEAR?"

There was silence. "I can't talk about an active investigation."

"There's a shaman here. He told me yesterday that the pipeline was a target."

"And why didn't you call that in?"

She wanted to say because she was on administrative leave.

"I did call it in. I left a message with your administrative assistant and I phoned Luke Forrest and told him. He said the Phoenix field office was aware that the pipeline system was a potential target."

"Next time speak to me directly."

"Yes, sir."

She thought she'd gotten through to the right people. Had she made another mistake?

She saw her position eroding like a tree undercut by floodwaters.

"Maybe I should just drive down there."

"No. I gave you an order. And, Rivas? Keep your head down and your mouth shut. Okay?"

She closed her mouth but then opened it again. Sophia regretted her words even as she spoke but she could not remain mute.

"The tribal council up here on Turquoise Canyon believes that BEAR will strike the reservoir system. Anytime now, since the first cell has hit their target."

"We don't know it's BEAR."

She did. She felt certain and until she had credible evidence to the contrary, she was sticking with that theory.

"Can you at least send up the National Guard?"

"Sophia, they're deploying the National Guard and every available law enforcement agency to Phoenix."

"Highway patrol?" she asked, her voice a croak.

She was met with silence.

"Larry?"

"Yes. Highway patrol, too. Listen. I got to go. Stay out of trouble up there." The line went dead.

Sophia stood there with the phone pressed to her ear, the line buzzing with her mind. They blew up the pipeline, just as Kenshaw Little Falcon had told her they would. And they would hit the reservoir, too. And if the larger Alchesay Dam was as poorly secured as Skeleton Cliff, it would make an easy target. Easier now if they also pulled the highway patrol.

She lowered the phone to its cradle and met

Jack's gaze. He was waiting for her. Waiting for the awesome weight of responsibility to settle over her. She could choose to do nothing, wait and see. If she did that, she might still be reinstated, but this place and his people might be washed away. Or she could act and lose everything.

"They pulled the highway patrol," she said.

Jack's forehead furrowed as his brows dipped low over troubled eyes.

"We should leave," she said.

"There are too many of us. Our senior center is in Piñon Forks. Our day care. Our schools. Our medical clinic. Our new woman's health center. Even if we got every single person clear, for how long? Days? Weeks? It's not possible."

She wanted to get him to leave with her but could not find the nerve to ask him.

"We can't leave," said Jack. "You can. You should."

He was trying to save her. Well, she was not leaving Jack Bear Den here to die. Even if he had tried to seduce her into staying. And it had worked, darn it.

"Take me to see Alchesay Dam."

The frown vanished. On the way she mentioned her reservations. Not the obvious ones, like losing her job, being arrested and prosecuted, and likely spending a very, very long time in a federal prison. No, she stuck to the practical.

THEY REACHED THE larger dam and power station by midmorning. She was relieved to see that Alchesay Dam was better guarded than Skeleton Cliff. They had the National Guard on site in plain view with the highway patrol. The barricades were larger than at Skeleton Cliff Dam and there was more than one. A truck or car could not gain access via the road that crossed the dam from either side.

The National Guard sat in a Humvee at the barricade before the power-station gate. In addition, there was a floating barricade on Goodwin Lake supported by a patrol boat ready to intercept any leisure boater who ventured too near.

Clearly they believed this was BEAR's target. What if the beefed-up security here actually served to make Jack's reservation more vulnerable?

If she was in charge of an attack, she would certainly move her aim to Skeleton Cliff and possibly Red Rock Dam below his reservation. Breaching them both might create enough hydraulic force from the released water in Canyon Lake and Two Mountain Lake to destroy the smaller Mesa Salado Dam. No question that the water would overflow. And with three power stations knocked out, the city would go dark. All those humming air conditioners, which made life in the desert possible, would go silent.

"We're on our own, you know," she said after scouting Red Rock Dam and finding it vulnerable. "No one is coming."

Sophia glanced at Jack. Last night she had thought that she had found a man who was different. He was strong and self-contained. He had purpose and vision. And it had all been an illusion. Had he used her to get this help, or had he been as moved as she was?

They needed to talk. Her about last night. Him about the personal bomb that just went off when she opened those test results. But that wouldn't happen because she needed to circle the wagons.

Regret scalded her. She wished, hoped… It didn't matter.

She'd come and consulted. Now it was time to go.

Nothing was going to stop her from getting through this inquiry and getting reinstated. Nothing. Not him. Not his tribe. Not the senior center that sat beside the river.

"How do I get the explosives to set up the blast?"

JACK HAD THE miners of Turquoise Canyon on the ridge site within the hour. They knew how to blast away a boulder and how to drill a hole for a charge. They did not know how to take down the tonnage needed to completely block the river and be strong enough to hold when the flood waters crashed against it. If the explosion went wrong, all they would do was add rolling jagged torpedoes of rock to the destructive force of the water.

Did Sophia have the expertise they needed?

Wallace Tinnin arrived as the men were drilling the holes in the rock.

He regarded the operation with hands on hips and the kind of grim acceptance he often used when facing an unpleasant task.

"Sorry I'm late. We have another report of a runaway."

Jack swiveled his head toward his chief. "Another since Kacy Doka?"

"Yeah. That's four."

"Another girl?" asked Jack.

Wallace nodded. "I've got a bad feeling. These girls aren't tied up with gangs. All I can find, they're sweet and never been in trouble."

"Their families?"

He looked toward the sky. "Awful. Single parent. Drug users. Drug suppliers. Multiple run-ins with us and outside law enforcement. I swear, some of them hardly noticed their kid was missing."

That made Jack's heart ache.

"I want you on this."

Jack rested his hands on his hips, considering his argument. He was not going to leave his escort duty, especially after the attack.

"But I'll send Redhorse out to do preliminaries for now. We need you here."

Jack nodded, his hands sliding to his sides.

"I spoke to Kenshaw," said Wallace. "Asked him if he knew his cell had been activated."

Jack lifted his brow. Kenshaw had told them

that his cell of BEAR had been assigned to the pipelines.

"He said he wasn't contacted," said Wallace.

Jack scowled. "You believe him?"

Wallace inclined his head.

"If what he said is true, then they know he's working with the Feds," said Jack.

"Looks that way."

"You think they'll try to get to him?"

"Maybe."

Jack added Kenshaw to the list of people needing protection.

Tinnin looked out at the men crawling over the rock.

"We got enough material?"

"We have the blasting caps, batteries and DET cord. She needed two burner phones. Those just arrived."

"She's not using shock tubing?" asked Wallace.

His chief's family had a claim, and his chief knew how to handle explosives.

"She said anyone could set that off. She wants full control. So she's using an electric initiator. I'm not sure about the main charge. She seems worried," said Jack. "She also wants everything we have left moved here to the station."

"Why?"

"To secure it, but also to have it close at hand, near the river."

The station was in tribal headquarters and sat across the street from the river. If they got much closer, they'd need the tribes' twenty-four-foot police boat.

"She's about to destroy her career. You know that, right? That hill goes boom and she's just another unemployed Indian, maybe one going to prison."

"We can protect her."

Tinnin didn't look convinced. "Maybe. She's on our land. Unfortunately the FBI thinks it's federal land."

He knew that. Knew the risk she was taking

and it made him sick. In spite of whatever he did, there were some things he couldn't keep from happening. His mind flashed back to Yeager Hatch, the comrade that none of them could reach in time.

Jack watched Sophia moving along the ridge. She progressed with an intensity of focus and alertness that he had not seen before. But he had not seen Sophia on the job until today.

The sun was descending toward the canyon ridge when she finally climbed up the rock to speak to them. The woman was as agile as a monkey.

"Almost done," she said. Her breathing was still heavy from her exertions. Sweat beaded on her brow and she worked to fill her lungs with air.

"The explosives are set in two separate sequences. The first will take down that lower section and the second will remove this ridge. They're going to feel it down in Piñon Forks. The debris will go a quarter mile, but shock waves will easily travel a mile. Might take out some windows."

"You think it's coming, don't you?" asked Jack.

"I wouldn't be up here if I didn't. I'd like to ask that your department help guard Skeleton Cliff Dam. Maybe we can stop them."

"Better to be proactive," said Wallace. "We've got Tribal Thunder watching the dam and we have snipers and drone surveillance. But we don't know when or how."

"Drones?" she asked.

"My son owns one," he said. "Short range. Good images, though, in real time."

She nodded.

"Any chance this will go off accidentally?" asked Jack.

"None. I trigger the blasts with this." She lifted her phone.

Jack was about to remind her that any of the miners would know how to bypass any initiator she devised when Tinnin interrupted.

"Couldn't anyone do it from over there?" Tinnin pointed toward the ridge.

"Anyone that wants to die. The shock wave from the blasts will kill anyone up here." She pointed over the cliff. "Or down there. You'd have to be that close to manually fire the blasting caps."

"That's your security system?" asked Jack. "You have to die to set them off?"

"No. If there was time, you could run additional nonel tubing. Get far enough away or behind adequate cover."

"I think we should run that cording now," said Jack.

"There is no adequate cover," she said.

"We have nonel tubing in thousand-yard rolls."

"Which we are securing at the station. Right?" she asked.

Tinnin nodded. "Yes, ma'am.

"You plan to set it off remotely, then?" Wallace asked Sophia.

"Yup. I'm using two burner phones and nine-volt batteries to boost the charge. Only I know the numbers for each phone and my phone is password protected."

Jack and Tinnin exchanged a look and Jack knew his chief was not happy that they could not initiate the blast without Sophia.

"If the dam goes, will we have time to trigger both blasts?" she asked.

"We've got eyes on the dam 24/7 and the power company has a siren they sound at noon and for emergencies."

Sophia surveyed her work and nodded. "I'm done here."

"All that's left is to pray we never have to place those two phone calls," said Tinnin.

Waiting, Jack realized, was going to be hell.

Chapter Fourteen

Sophia and Jack reached Piñon Forks after dark, hot, dusty and thirsty. The cool interior of the tribe's casino bar welcomed as they arrived with ten minutes to spare before the happy hour food specials ended. He picked a booth and asked for menus. She studied hers and he lowered his to the table. He had to be starving, she thought, because they had missed lunch.

"You already know what you want?" she asked.

"Got it memorized."

When the waitress returned, he asked for water and then ordered chicken wings, south-west egg rolls and cheesy spinach dip. He asked Sophia to choose a drink and she picked soda, thinking she could use the sugar rush after the exertions of the day.

The waitress made an efficient turn and retreated toward the bar to get her soda.

"You don't drink?" he asked.

"Mom has a problem with alcohol." Among other things. "I figure I won't risk it."

Jack nodded. Alcoholism ran in families and she'd wager he'd seen his share of drunken brawls, domestic violence and the removal of a child or two from reckless endangerment or neglect. She rubbed her forehead, trying not to go back there in her mind. Still, she thought she heard her mother screaming at the cops and her husband and her kids.

Sophia thought she was doing so well. She didn't often think of the home she'd left. Home. She snorted. If you could call it that.

Her siblings had been scattered by the foster care system or their own sadness. She didn't know her older siblings, Brenda or Amanda. They were taken before she had memory of them. She recalled Marvin and Velma and when Wilbur was born, though she'd not yet been two. How many did her mother have now? She doubted Vera even knew. None of her siblings had tried to find her and she had not tried to find them.

The drinks arrived. She finished hers before Jack had even taken a sip.

"You okay?"

"Yeah." She said it automatically, as people do when someone asks how they're doing. *Fine. And you?*

Not fine. Not okay.

She scoured the menu, already knowing what she was having but needing the privacy the shiny laminated booklet allowed.

Oh, no, her eyes were not tearing up. She refused to allow it. Sophia dragged in a breath and blew it away.

Jack placed one finger on the menu and

pushed it to the table, pinning it beneath his index finger. She glanced up to find concern in his eyes.

"Sophia?"

"Was Ray right, Jack?" she asked. "Did you sleep with me to get my help?"

The waitress returned with the appetizers and asked if they'd made up their minds. She ordered a burger and sweet potato fries. Jack told her he'd have the same, mostly, Sophia believed, to be rid of her.

Jack pushed the egg rolls in her direction.

She glanced from the peace offering back to him, waiting.

"No. He wasn't right. Sophia, you don't know me that well, but I'm not like that. I don't use women."

"I think you just did."

"You said you'd help us."

He was right. Much as she'd love to put this on him, she'd set the charges and laid the fuse.

"So I did. Amazing what bad choices I've made since coming here."

He looked away. Seemed he didn't like being labeled a bad choice. He faced her again just a moment later. The man was either a sucker for punishment or as strong as he looked.

"Sophia, I know you came up here to give an opinion. I know that getting involved with me and that ridge line were not in your plans. But what you did for us today—I hope we never need it, but if we do, it might save us all."

"*If* it works. There's no guarantee it will. I've never set an explosion even a third that big." Was she actually excited at the prospect of seeing if those charges would block the river?

"I'm only staying until the pipeline is secured and they can increase security up here."

"I understand."

She reached for a neatly sliced half of the egg roll that oozed cheese and hot chili.

"I have a life down there in the valley. I've made a life and I am not coming back to the rez to live on my portion of the per capita payments from the tribal trust. I don't need it."

"That's your prerogative," he said.

She felt a bubble of pain in her throat. She couldn't swallow. Sophia dropped the untouched appetizer back to the plate.

Jack reached across the table and took both her hands.

"Sophia, you're saving us."

"Maybe so. But when they find out, they'll terminate me. Ask for my shield. How would that make you feel, Jack?"

He drew back. "It was a lot to ask. Too much, maybe. But I'd ask again. I'd have to. We have no choice. If we believe Kenshaw, we have to act."

The burgers arrived. Sophia choked down what she could. Jack finished his burger first, of course, and offered her the wings. When she declined, he polished them off, too, along with the remains of the egg rolls. The man could eat, but judging from his size, he needed to.

The waitress checked in and finally cleared away the plates.

"Y'all save room for dessert?"

She shook her head and Jack looked disappointed when he asked for the check.

They settled up and headed out. Jack waved to the patrol car waiting in the lot.

"You have them following us?" she asked.

"Seems prudent after yesterday."

Was that only yesterday that someone had taken a shot at her? It seemed days ago.

He held open the door to his white truck and she slipped into the passenger seat.

"My grandfather says 'don't borrow trouble,'" said Jack. "But my dad says 'when you have trouble, go help someone with theirs.'"

"I think that is why my cousin, Luke, sent me up here."

"I was talking about my troubles, Sophia."

He stood beside her seat in the space beside the open passenger door to his truck, shifting as if trying to get comfortable in his own skin.

"I want you to come with me to see my folks. I need some answers."

He had dear friends in Dylan and Ray. He had a twin brother just returned from witness protection. Yet he did not ask them to come with him. He asked her.

"Why me?"

"Sophia, I've been an outsider here all my life. Seems like you know something about how that feels."

"But they love you. Have accepted you."

"And, if those results are correct, they have lied to me since I was born. I want to know why."

JACK TRIED TO stand still as he waited for Sophia to respond to his request, but he couldn't help but weave like a snake to the sound of the flute. It wasn't the sort of thing you asked a woman whom you had known only a few days. But it seemed so much longer and his knowledge of her so much deeper. Perhaps it was the crucible of danger, but she had risen in his estimation each hour of each day.

At last she nodded, accepting his request to come with him. It was Sunday night. They'd be home, all of them except Thomas, who had returned to the border south of Lilac with the Shadow Wolves.

It wasn't far from the casino to Piñon Forks, where his parents lived. Just a short drive along the river that had changed from friend to enemy in the last few months. They were at the modest home of his birth far too soon. He pulled up on the flat pad, extended by his father because his boys all drove trucks and mostly came home for supper on Sundays.

Jack pulled past Kurt's blue Ram pickup, parking beside Carter's red F-150. Carter liked red because he was a Hotshot, fighting wildfires all over the west. In fact, he had been captain of the tribe's team, the Turquoise Canyon Hotshots. But Ray had taken his place during his absence and done a great job, by all accounts. Jack wondered who would lead now.

Jack turned off the engine and the truck fell silent.

Sophia sat quietly beside him in the dark.

"Changing your mind or just gathering your nerve?" she asked.

"Neither. I'm reconsidering you witnessing this."

She had just met his family and he did not want his second visit to be unpleasant. He didn't know why it was important for them to like her and for her to like them, but it was.

He pressed his hand to his forehead as understanding dawned. He'd brought Sophia to meet his parents at their home. The first girl and the first time. Only he'd disguised the visit even from himself because he knew she wasn't staying, despite their obvious compatibility in the sack.

"You worried I will think badly of them because they kept this secret from you?"

He lowered his head, not knowing what he thought or what he wanted. Answers, he supposed. Something to fill up this empty hole in his chest he carried day in and day out.

"It might be rough," he said and lowered his hands to grip the wheel of his vehicle, as if already planning his getaway.

She made a sound that might have been a laugh. Jack turned in the seat to look at her. The light from the living room filtered out through closed curtains and illuminated the yard in yellow light. He could see Sophia's face in shadows and she was smiling.

"Jack, I'm going to say this quick, because when you uncover a wound, it's best to get that Band-Aid off as fast as possible."

He tensed, bracing for whatever she would say.

"You are supposed to honor your parents. I mostly avoid mine. I don't visit my father." She laughed. "Though I might see him real soon if I have to trigger that blast."

Did she mean her father was still in prison and that she would be joining him? He wanted to ask but did not want to interrupt.

"My mom still lives up there on Black Mountain rez. But she isn't well. Too many years of hard drinking. But I'm still lucky. You want to know why?"

He nodded.

"Because she had me early and I'm not like my younger brothers—Ned and Talbert both have fetal alcohol syndrome. And they didn't have my grandmother, not for long. I had one good loving parent in my grandma, and I had an excellent example of why I needed to get my degree, keep my 18 Money and get off the rez. I can't thank my mother enough for that. Now, I only just met your folks. But I know they love you. They'll have a good reason, Jack. Let's go find out what it is."

She didn't wait, just threw open the passenger door and slipped out. A moment later she was holding open his door and motioning to the yard.

"I won't be embarrassed, Jack. But I'll be there for you. You give me the sign and I'll take you out of there."

Funny, to look at them, you'd assume he was the strong one. But it was Sophia who had the backbone needed to get answers, because she'd faced far worse. He knew too many girls who had similar upbringings that had not done so well. Five of them were missing right now. Tinnin had told him he'd assigned their new man, Jake Redhorse, to look into the disappearances. Jack felt he should be investigating, but both he and his chief believed that the threat from BEAR and protecting Sophia from possible gang attacks took precedence.

Sophia held out her hand. He took it. They walked hand-in-hand up to the front door. He reached for the knob and she grabbed his wrist.

"Wait!" There was a note of panic in her voice.

"What?" he asked.

"I forgot your mother's first name."

She looked so worried it struck him as comical. His entire life had been a lie and here she was worried about this?

"Annetta. And he's Delane. Brothers are Carter, Kurt and Thomas. Thomas won't be here."

"Back on the border. Got it." Her hand dropped to her side.

He was still smiling when he opened the door. If she didn't care about him, it wouldn't be important to know those names. She said she was leaving and didn't want any attachments. But she acted as if she did.

His mother spotted him first. "Well, Jack! This is a surprise. Look at you two, all dusty." She swept forward and kissed him, and then kissed Sophia. "We just finished dinner but I can heat up the casserole. Are you hungry?"

"We just ate, Mom."

"Oh, that's a shame. Just some dessert then?

I have pumpkin pie, lemon cake or chocolate ice cream." She waited for them to choose, ready to dart into the kitchen and fix them something.

They left the entrance, his mother leading the way, and paused in the small living room. Carter waved from the sagging sofa where he sat beside Amber.

In the living room the ballgame blared as the Diamondbacks took on the Padres. His father lowered the sound and stood to greet them. Kurt sat on the couch, closest to the set, with Carter's wife in the middle between her brother-in-law and her new husband. Amber placed a bookmark in the novel she read, waiting for Kurt to rise so she could clear the coffee table to greet them.

"We just…" Jack's words failed him.

His father looked from him to Sophia.

"They're not here for dessert," said his dad.

"What happened?" asked his mother, dessert forgotten for the moment. Her hands laced before her, gripping tight as if preparing to pray on a moment's notice.

Carter rose to his feet. He was a big man and he wore his hair in the fashion Jack admired— long, loose and, of course, straight. He stepped clear of the coffee table. Amber trailed behind him, blending seamlessly into his family as if she had always been here.

"You opened it," said Carter.

Jack nodded.

"Opened what?" asked their mother.

Carter stared at him as if trying to learn what he had discovered with a look. Jack reached in his wallet and passed him the wrinkled, torn envelope. Carter held it as if Jack had just served him a subpoena.

"What's going on?" His mother's clasped hands had now reached her throat. "What is that? Is it from the marines?"

His mother's biggest fear was that her boys would be called back overseas by the marines.

Carter was now scanning the page.

Jack couldn't find his voice to ask the questions. His throat was burning and tight. He looked to Sophia.

"Me?" she asked.

He nodded and she gave his hand a quick squeeze.

"They're test results, Mrs. Bear Den."

His mother's hands pressed flat over her chest. "Jack, are you ill? You're so pale."

His father stepped up to support his mother, holding on to her elbow and draping one arm around her lower back.

"He's not ill. No one is," Sophia assured them.

"What is all this?" asked his father.

"It's a sibling DNA test," said Sophia. "Jack and Carter sent a sample to see if they shared the same genetic markers."

Now his mother had gone pale.

"Why would you do that?" asked his father.

"I knew it," whispered his mother. "I knew."

Knew what, he wanted to ask, but here, now

all he could do was stand mutely by and wait for Sophia to ask the next question.

"Let's go sit down," said his dad, escorting his wife to the dining room and a seat. He did not take his place at the head of the long rectangular table, but slid into the adjoining bench beside Annetta.

The family all took their places, with Jack sitting in the chair belonging to his father. Sophia sat to his right. Carter dropped the damning evidence on the table and took his seat, and Amber and Kurt joined them a moment later.

Sophia looked to his parents as she spoke. "Jack is interested to know why he was not told that he is not your child, but rather a nephew to one of you. Could you explain that, please?"

Chapter Fifteen

Sophia felt like the rain cloud pouring down on this wonderful family. Carter, Jack and Kurt all stared at their parents with looks of utter astonishment.

Annetta sat ramrod-straight with her husband's hand still pressed to her lower back. Tears coursed down her cheeks, but her chin had taken on a defiant tilt.

"You are my son."

Jack and Carter shared a look that seemed to involve some silent communication all their own. Sophia returned her focus to Annetta, waiting. She'd interviewed enough suspects to know when one had not finished speaking.

"But…" Annetta said.

Here it comes, thought Sophia. Jack reached under the table and squeezed her knee so tightly she flinched. She slipped her hand into his, mainly as self-defense to keep him from crushing her kneecap.

"But you were born to my older sister, Ava."

Kurt said, "I didn't know you had a sister."

"She had to leave," said Annetta. "She saw something terrible, a murder." She looked at Jack now with such sorrow that Sophia found herself squeezing Jack's hand. "Your father's murder. He died before you were even born."

Jack's jaw went to granite.

Annetta's shoulders slumped and Delane took over like a relay runner relieving a teammate.

"Your father's name was Robert Taaga. Your mother called him Robbie. He was Hawaiian. A really big guy."

"They met in Phoenix," said Annetta. "He was going to the university, too. Classmates.

He was helping her get through physics. So smart. She said he was so smart."

So Jack had gotten his size and features from a man of South Pacific descent. Sophia had seen some pro athletes and actors who were Samoans, and they had been epic in size, like Jack. And his father had been murdered.

Annetta was shaking her head and staring vacantly at a spot before her on the table.

"What happened?" asked Carter.

Their father answered. "There was a robbery attempt. Robbie stepped in. Ava said they shot him the minute that he took a step in their direction. Even with two bullets in his heart, he still got the killer's gun."

Sophia imagined Jack's strong heart trying to beat against the blood loss and the picture in her mind washed her cold.

"Ava saw both attackers. She made a positive ID, she testified and sent them both to prison, but they were in a gang and the Justice Department said they wouldn't stop. That the gang would send a message by killing Ava if they could," said Delane. He blew out a breath. "Your mom did not want you raised out there. She wanted you to know your people and your tribe. So she made a hard choice. She asked Annetta to raise you as her boy."

But how had they managed to keep this secret? The tribe must have known or at least suspected.

"She made it a condition of her cooperation. They were both pregnant at the same time. Annetta with Carter and Ava with Jack. So when Ava delivered, they brought us to her. We said we were visiting my brother in Fort Collins, Colorado. He was on a survey crew up there for an oil and gas company. We left and we didn't come back until you were born, Carter." Delane looked to his oldest son.

And then they brought home the twins that were not twins. Three sons, Sophia realized. Not four.

"You were so tiny," Delane said to Carter, measuring the distance with his hands.

"He was not," said Annetta. "He weighed six pounds, six ounces."

"But Jack was two months old by then, and he was over nine pounds when he was born. Our twins came home and Annetta kept you both close."

"People must have known," said Sophia.

"They did, some anyway."

But this was a tribe, Sophia thought, and not like Black Mountain, with several towns and so many members spread out over so much land that it would be impossible to know everyone. But here they did know everyone and everyone knew how to keep a secret, especially an important one. And they kept it even from Carter and Jack.

Jack looked at his twin.

"We're not brothers," said Jack, the pain raw in his voice.

Carter reached across the corner of the table

that separated them and pulled Jack close. The hug was fierce and possessive.

"We are. We are."

Kurt stood and joined the two. The rest of them all seemed to hold collective breath. Finally Jack pulled away.

"You guys are wrinkling my shirt." His shirt was filthy with dirt and dust, so his comment broke the tension and made everyone laugh.

"Let me up," said Annetta to Delane. She stood. "I have to get some things for Jack."

They sat waiting for her return, hearing her thumping around the bedroom down the hall.

"I can't see her?" said Jack to his father, meaning Ava, Sophia was sure.

He shook his head.

"Call or write?" he asked.

"Talk to your friend Agent Forrest. Maybe he can arrange something. They haven't let us see her. We don't know a thing except that she's alive. Nothing, for all these years. But she knows about you, Jack."

Sophia's brow wrinkled. That wasn't possible.

"The classifieds," said Jack.

Delane smiled. "That's why you're the detective. Yes. She and her sister worked it out. Ava can go online and read the news. Classifieds are always in there. She's let her know you played baseball and when you graduated from school. That you were safe after your tours of duty. Something on your birthday—the one we picked for you both. Right between February 2nd and April 2nd."

Carter and Jack stared, realizing they had been celebrating the wrong birthday their entire lives.

"I'm keeping it," said Carter.

"Me, too," said Jack.

Annetta returned with a shoe box.

"This was my sister's. I kept them for you even though they told me not to. That I should destroy anything that would reveal who you were. She made me promise never to tell you,

Jack. I promised her the day you were born. I didn't lie about you being my son. You are mine as much as you are hers. And I told the truth when I said I'd never been with a man other than my husband. But I didn't tell you that you were Ava's child before you were mine. I promised her, Jack. I'm sorry."

Because she was protecting him, and Sophia saw exactly why keeping that secret was so important. Suddenly Jack rose to his feet.

"What was the name of the man who shot my father?"

"He's in federal prison. Life sentence."

"The name?"

Delane shook his head. Sophia knew that Jack could find the information easily. Everyone did, but still the name was not coming from his parents.

"Before you run off after him," said Kurt, "maybe you should remember your promise to Kenshaw, and that BEAR just blew up a pipeline in Phoenix and that we are probably next."

Jack sat back down in front of the box Annetta had left him. Carter pressed a hand to his back, high up, directly over the medicine wheel. Was Carter reminding Jack to use the wheel to help find his direction?

Jack blew out a breath and then lifted the old box from the table, as if it was fragile, like an eggshell. He tucked it under his arm and looked to Sophia.

"We need to go."

"Jack, don't run off," said Annetta.

"I'm not going after him, Mom. I just need some time to…" He looked at Sophia. "You ready?"

She followed him out of his parents' house with his family trailing as far as the front steps. Sophia held out her hand.

"Keys," she said.

He turned them over without a word of objection. She had the seat adjusted by the time he was belted into his.

"Where to?" she asked, backing them out.

"I'd prefer to be in Piñon Forks in case something happens."

She headed toward the town.

"You said the casino hotel is closed for reno."

"We're going to my place."

She saw the squad car on the shoulder. It pulled out as they passed.

"One of your men?" she asked.

"Hmm?" He turned to glance out the side mirror. "Yeah. That's Wetselline. He's our shadow tonight."

She had not seen him on their way from the canyon and that bothered her. Jack was a distraction and she was getting all tied up in his problems. It had made her forget her own, just as Luke had promised. She had never been so completely overtaken by anything other than her job in years. She didn't like it. Didn't like that being with Jack was more appealing than returning to her position and that the problems on Turquoise Canyon were becoming her problems. Somewhere along the way in the consultation, she had taken a wrong turn. She needed to get back home to her job and her life.

Jack thanked her for coming with him.

She made the obligatory reply and flicked on the radio to static.

"Local station goes off at seven."

"I have to get out of here," she said. But instead she drove to Jack's place. Not because it was closer to the dam and got better mobile phone service, but because whether she would admit it aloud or not, she wanted to be here with Jack.

Chapter Sixteen

Sophia sat beside Jack on the couch of his comfortable ranch-style house. He had too much black leather furniture and not enough food in the refrigerator, but the space was clean. She especially liked the wall decorations. Instead of paintings, he had hung various drums. Some were elaborately adorned art pieces and others looked ancient, with rawhide heads so thin the center of the leather was transparent.

Jack had been exceedingly quiet on the ride to his place. "Your things are in the spare room. I had Ray bring them over."

She slipped a hand onto his knee. It was obvious he was feeling lost and the confusion was etched in lines across his forehead.

"It's not what you expected. Is it?" she asked.

He shook his head. "I… I'm just… Am I supposed to get a surfboard now? I've never even seen the Pacific Ocean."

"You don't need to do anything except keep the secret that your family has kept for you. They were protecting you."

"But all this time. They wouldn't still be after her."

"Gang hits have no expiry date. Once you are targeted that target stays on your back unless they withdraw it."

And now Sophia had the same target on her back, as his mother had once had. Would they take her into protective custody, too?

"She should have taken me with her."

"Is that what you would have done, in her place?"

He sighed.

"She might be living in Detroit or Dallas.

She's cut off from her family and friends. And she did nothing wrong. It was just really horrible luck," she said.

"I knew I was different, that we had different fathers."

"And mothers. That's the surprise. But you still have Annetta. She's more mother than many."

"I feel sick," he said.

"Take some time. Time helps." She knew something else that would help ease his mind, soothe his body. Sophia admitted the truth, she was not some angel of mercy. She wanted Jack again. It was possible that the investigation on her use of force might take longer than usual because of the pipeline explosion. Or it might be expedited for the same reason. And if they ruled in her favor, she'd be back on the job. She looped her arm around Jack's stronger one and lay her head on his shoulder.

"You can't change it."

"Change what?"

"The past. I've been trying to bury mine. You've been trying to uncover yours. Uncovered or ignored, it's still there like an infection in your jaw. Eventually you have to deal with it."

He turned to her. "But not tonight."

Her body tingled with anticipation as he leaned in and kissed her, slow and deep. She laced her fingers around his neck and he eased her down to the thick leather cushions of his couch.

"I need you, Sophia," he whispered, hot breath fanning the hair at her neck.

"Me, too." How had this happened? She should be keeping her distance. Reminding him that she was here only to give her opinion and to distract herself from the investigation.

Well, Jack was the best darn distraction she'd ever had. And when his hands covered her breasts, she ached to have those big hands pressed to her bare skin.

She unclipped her holster and slipped out

of it and her blazer. Then she unbuttoned her blouse. His mouth found the bare skin at her stomach, traveling up as she released each button. Then he pushed the fabric off her shoulders. She sat up and he let her go. Sophia did not know where she got the nerve, but Jack's hungry eyes made her bold. So she dropped her blouse and released her bra, letting them fall to the floor. Then she slipped out of her shoes and slacks. She stood in only her panties. Jack sat on the edge of the couch, both hands on the couch cushions as his gaze devoured her.

"So beautiful," he whispered.

She hooked a thumb in the elastic of her panties and lowered them over her hips, then kicked them away.

Sophia stood wearing only a smile. Their eyes met.

"Your turn, Jack."

He rose from the couch like a charging bull, but instead of disrobing he lifted her up into his arms and ran her toward the back of the house.

She squealed as he tossed her onto his bed and then flicked on the light on the side table.

"I never do this," he said.

"I think you did this last night."

"I mean here. I don't bring women here. I don't bring them to meet my parents, either."

"Why not?"

"Never found one I liked that much. Didn't want to give them the wrong idea."

"But I'm safe. Right? Because I'm leaving."

"No, Sophia. You're dangerous because I don't want you to leave."

The smile left her.

"Jack, I have to go. You know that."

"I do. It makes this sweeter and sadder."

This was a bad idea. The man had been left behind by his mother and now she was preparing to do exactly the same thing. Sleeping with Jack wouldn't make him feel better. Not in the long run, because whatever was happening between them, it was growing stronger. Just the thought of leaving him made her chest ache. But she could no more leave his bed right now than she could stop breathing.

Sophia extended her hand. "Come to bed, Jack."

SOPHIA WAS STILL ASLEEP. They had spent much of the night tangled in each other's arms, sharing the passion that seemed to burn between them like wildfire. But well before the dawn, he woke, his mind racing with his heart. He needed to see what his mother had left him. So he rose and headed for the kitchen and then out to the concrete drive and his truck. He returned to the dark kitchen with the shoe box and flicked on the light. Then he sat alone at the kitchen table.

Inside were photos he had never seen. Photos of two sisters. The photos of the sisters as young women showed the differences. His mother, Ava, the oldest, was smaller than Annetta. Ironic, he thought, as he studied each image of his mother. Maybe he'd see her sometime, someplace. Unexpectedly. But she was now twenty-eight years older. What did she look like now?

There was a diary, written by his mother. He did the math and realized she began the entries at fifteen and continued on and off into her first year of college. He flipped to the end and saw his father's name written out in bold letters:

Robbie Taaga and I went to the movies. I really like him. When I'm with him I'm so happy and when we are apart I hurt inside.

Jack lowered the book. He had not been away from Sophia. But just the prospect of her departure filled him with gloom. Was it because of all this? Maybe this was about his mother leaving and not Sophia at all.

He closed the diary and placed it carefully back in the box. It wasn't about the past. He was now haunted by the future. What would happen if that dam broke? What would happen if she left them before the strike? He knew the attack was coming. He believed Kenshaw Little Falcon's prediction that the dam, their dam, was the new prime target of one of the cells.

So why did he want to follow Sophia back to Flagstaff when she left them? His life, his duty and the legacy his mother had given him were all here. But soon Sophia would not be.

"Hey, there," she said.

Her voice had been just a whisper but he still startled.

"Sorry," she said.

"Didn't hear you."

"I was standing here awhile. You seemed lost in thought."

She stood in bare feet in a familiar flannel robe. It belonged to him and reached nearly to her toes. It also gaped at the chest, revealing a wide swath of smooth skin and the curves of her breasts.

"Borrowed this." She tugged at the worn collar.

"It never looked so good."

She came forward, stood just behind him with a hand on his shoulder. "Interesting?"

He handed her an envelope he had not yet opened marked *Jack*.

She slipped into the seat next to him and opened the flap.

"Photos," she said, flipping rapidly through the stack, her smile growing wider until she grinned. "These are precious."

She moved to sit on his lap and she went through the pictures again for him. It was his mother, pregnant. Then in a hospital bed, with circles under Ava's eyes, smiling joyfully as she held a dark-headed baby. Beside her bed was Annetta, obviously pregnant as well. What she saw as happy, he saw as sad. One of the photos showed a guard at the door. It was the last time he would ever see his mother, and he could not remember her face.

"Can you find her?" he asked.

She stilled and then lowered the photos to the table surface.

"Perhaps. But it would put her in danger."

"Why? Anyone who is still looking for her would not know she has a son."

"That's true. I'll see what I can arrange." She glanced toward the stove and the digital clock there. "Too early to call. Coffee?" she asked.

"All ready. Just hit the switch."

Sophia flipped on the drip coffeemaker and left him, heading for the bathroom and a shower. Jack put away the box. Sophia might be able to arrange a meeting. He felt butterflies in his belly at the thought. He wanted to meet her, but what if she was disappointed in him?

Sophia called to him. When he reached the bathroom, he opened the door enough to peek inside. She asked him to come in and he did. The view of Sophia's naked, soapy body through the textured glass was something he would never forget.

"Come in before the water gets cold."

As it turned out, the water did get cold before they left the shower's stream. His legs were trembling and her smile curled his toes. Sophia was generous and inventive and full of surprises. He toweled her dry, which started them off again, and they ended tangled up in damp towels and sheets in his bed. They dozed with Sophia's warm clean body draped across him until his phone woke them.

He lifted the mobile and saw it was Wallace Tinnin and that it was after nine on a Monday morning.

"Yeah, Chief," he said.

"You coming in?"

He was generally there by eight.

"On my way."

"Listen, we got something on Trey."

Tinnin was speaking about the gangbanger

Jack had picked up. The one who had used his one phone call to reveal Sophia's location.

"Minnie said that Trey got a video on his phone. He showed it to her. I've got his phone and I watched it. It's a carjacking and Sophia is the driver of the car. She's clearly visible and they recorded the shooting."

It was on the phone of Trey Fields. Why?

"Minnie said there was a still photo, too. Can't find that. Might have been deleted. But Minnie says it was an Instagram shot made up to look like a wanted poster with Sophia's image. Minnie said they don't know her name. Just that she killed one of their guys."

"He recognized her when I arrested him," said Jack.

"Seems so."

Jack had put Sophia in danger by making that collar. He'd seen Fields and just reacted. But he was supposed to be escorting Sophia. She was law enforcement so he had not considered any consequences of involving her.

"Who did he call?" asked Jack.

"A friend here on Turquoise Canyon. Real question is, who did the friend call?"

"I'm bringing her into the station now," said Jack.

"Seems prudent," said Wallace. "I've alerted our guys to keep an eye out for suspicious persons."

"Wearing yellow and black," said Jack.

"Yeah. They know."

Jack disconnected and set the phone aside.

"So they know where I am," she said.

"It's not safe for you here anymore." So soon. His mind was screaming for him to stop her, keep her. Too soon, she would be leaving him, too soon.

They were up and dressed in record time, all business now as if the night and morning had happened in some different place to two different people.

"I wish I could stay awhile," she said in the truck.

Like forever, he thought.

"Yeah."

Her phone chimed. She slipped the mobile from her pocket and glanced at the screen.

"My captain," she said and took the call.

Jack could hear her captain through the speaker because his voice boomed. So he heard the conversation.

Her captain had good news. They had expedited the investigation and ruled the shooting justified. He was ordering her to report to Phoenix and the pipeline explosion ASAP.

She glanced at Jack. They both knew that she had set the explosives so that only she could trigger the blasts. Of course, his miners could bypass the system she set with time. If they had time.

Sophia told her boss the new developments.

Her captain swore. "Sit tight. You'll need an escort."

"Will do."

She disconnected and glanced to him. Had she intentionally bought them time?

"Justified," she said, then closed her eyes and sank into the passenger seat. "They ruled justified," she whispered.

The relief she expected never came. Instead she felt a kind of tearing inside her chest. It came with the words whispered in her soul… *now you must leave him.*

No. Not until she was sure he'd be safe.

"They'll still be looking for you," Jack said.

"Up here. Not in Phoenix. You said yourself, they don't know my name."

"That information could be wrong. I'm not betting your life on it."

"We better go," she said. Her throat squeezed so she said no more.

As they reached the station, Sophia received another call from her captain, Larry Burton.

"Highway patrol found the older brother of Martin Nequam. Juaquin is being detained on a gun charge."

"Rifle?" asked Sophia.

"Yup. And a handgun. They found a rifle with scope in his trunk."

Sophia blew out a breath.

Burton continued. "We're sending an escort to retrieve you."

Sophia's heart sped. She couldn't leave Turquoise Canyon now. The pipeline was a forensic investigation. But the threat here could still be prevented.

"I can't come back right now," she said and then held her breath at the audacity of her words. She had never refused an order before.

"What did you say?"

"I can't. There is a credible threat up here. We need more agents on Turquoise Canyon. Not less."

"Sophia, we have multiple explosions down here. You're an expert. I'm ordering you to report."

"Requesting personal leave, sir."

"Denied."

She closed her eyes and pictured everything she fought so hard to win destroyed by her own undermining. Then she looked at Jack's strong, solemn face.

"You'll have my resignation today, sir."

"What?" he howled.

Sophia disconnected and met Jack's gaze.

"That was the bravest thing I've ever seen."

"I'm a fool," she said.

"No. You're a warrior. And you just might have saved us all."

"What if your shaman is wrong? What if the dams are well protected or not even a target?"

"You saw the protection. And we are a target."

She nodded. "I know it."

Chapter Seventeen

Sophia had been singled out for a hit by the Latin Kings thanks to the work of Martin's brother, Juaquin. They had not figured out that she was FBI, but they knew she was on Turquoise Canyon. Just outside Tinnin's office, Jack called Luke Forrest and told him what was happening—the attempted hit, the death order, Sophia's resignation and the threat they still faced from BEAR.

The agent didn't take it well. But he could not come riding up the mountain to the rescue. There was too much chaos down in Phoenix. It was all over the news. Scenes of gas explosions and fireballs. Neighborhoods destroyed. Industrial parks in flames.

"You going to be able to keep her safe?" asked Luke.

"I'll protect her with my life," Jack said.

"Not what I asked," said Luke.

"Yes, I'll keep her safe. I swear."

On the other end of the phone there was a deep sigh. "Let me speak to her."

Jack passed off the phone and Sophia pressed the phone to her ear.

"Hi, Luke," she said.

Jack felt sick and proud all at once. She was staying. Was it because of him or them? Or did she just see the need of protecting his tribe? Some deep animal part of him wanted it to be because of him.

Sophia was Western Apache and exactly the sort of woman he always wanted and never felt he deserved, because he was different. Now he knew why and he wasn't certain that knowledge changed anything.

"I understand," she said. "Yes, I'm sure. I know what I'm doing."

Most Apache women he knew stayed on the reservation, close to their families, their language and their culture. Sophia had broken free, left her tribe and made a life for herself down in the desert. And she had thrown it all away for this.

He'd never be able to repay her, but he hoped she'd let him try.

Tinnin met Jack's gaze. His worried face told Jack that his chief wasn't sure they could handle what was coming. He motioned toward his office and Jack followed, leaving Sophia in the outer office on the phone.

"Will it work?" he asked Jack, motioning his head toward the river.

"I hope we never find out."

"She can't stay forever," he said. "Eventually she will have to show one of us how to trigger the blasts."

"That was a condition of her supervision."

"But our guys can bypass the ignition system she set up."

"I'm not sure they can. I wouldn't want to mess with the ignition system. It might blow up before the dam is damaged."

"I don't like it. What if one of those gang members gets by us and kills her?"

Jack's body surged to life at the hypothetical, preparing to fight. "We have to keep her safe."

"For how long, Jack? Protection detail is straining our resources. I need you on the runaways."

Jack's curiosity was piqued. "Did someone else go missing?"

"Yes, Lawrence Kesselman's kid."

"Which one? He has—what? Thirteen?"

"It's Maggie. She disappeared yesterday."

"How old?"

"Fourteen. She's the youngest to go missing. The others were between sixteen and eighteen."

Jack glanced to Sophia, who was still on the

phone, and then to his boss. "How's Jake Redhorse doing with the investigation?"

"He's fine, but he's not you," said the chief.

Tinnin was putting him between a rock and a hard place. The crimes on Turquoise Canyon did not stop because of the outside threat. If anything, Jack's inattention to his normal rounds had allowed crime to increase. The stack of paperwork on his desk was rising. He needed to get back to work and he needed to protect Sophia.

"I'll check in with Redhorse. See what he's got so far."

"Do that," said Tinnin.

Jack turned his back on his chief and walked away making a mental note to speak to Redhorse as he worried about the missing teens. Right now he needed to focus on BEAR. If Sophia was willing to risk everything to protect them from the river, he would do the same.

Jack returned to the squad room and his desk, taking a seat before the stack of unreturned messages. Sophia was off the phone and he was on his computer answering his email. She took a seat beside his desk.

"Funny," she said. "You have too much to do and I have not enough."

"That's a good thing," he said and smiled. But it wasn't. They decided it was best for her to stay here, close to the river and the protection of the squad room.

He took her with him in the afternoon to speak to two witnesses in one of his open cases, but he could not go on calls where she might be exposed or in danger. That evening, they ate together at his home in a kind of pall.

"This is bad," she said. "I don't want the dams to go. But I can't stay up here indefinitely."

But she now had nowhere else to go. He knew she would not return to her tribe. He wanted her to stay here with him, but how did he ask her that? She was an FBI agent, or she had been.

"How did you leave it with your captain?" Jack asked. He wanted her to choose him out of love, not need.

"He gave me one day to report. After that I'm insubordinate."

"I'm so sorry, Sophia, for dragging you into this and so grateful you are here to help us."

"I keep thinking of those explosives on that beautiful ridge. You understand that some of the rocks will fly over a mile and rain down over Piñon Forks. It will damage cars, buildings and people who don't take cover."

"The tribal council has the word out. The warning sirens mean take cover. Not evacuate."

"But what if I figured wrong? What if the blast is too small or too big or it doesn't completely stop the flood?"

"You set the charges, Sophia. What do you think will happen?"

"I've never set one that big."

"The miners were there. They tell me you

got it right, exploited every fault and fissure. It will work, Sophia."

Sophia's mobile phone rang and she glanced at the screen. "It's Luke." She stood as she took the call, as if coming to attention in front of a superior officer as she spoke her greeting.

Sophia listened for a few moments then glanced at Jack and excused herself, stepping away from the table and disappearing down the hallway to take her call. She returned a few minutes later and stood beside him at his dining room table.

"What's up?" asked Jack.

"He's worried about me."

"Understandable," he said.

"Let's go sit in the living room," Sophia said. She offered her hand and he grasped it, allowing her to lead him along to the leather sofa. He sat closest to the arm and she in the center, half turned to face him. He found his fingers gripping into the soft padding as he braced for whatever was troubling her.

"I asked him about your mom earlier today. He was getting back to me with some information."

Jack stiffened as hope mingled with dread. Was his mother alive? Was she safe?

"He couldn't get much out of his guy at the Justice Department. But he did find out that your mother is alive and living somewhere in the Midwest. Your mother is employed and she has remarried."

Jack pressed a hand flat on the armrest as his other hand squeezed the cushion edge flat. His mother had started again. Started a new family.

"She has children, Jack. You have sisters. He couldn't find out how many or their ages."

Sophia slipped from the sofa and kneeled before him, taking his hands in hers. "You have sisters, Jack! More than one."

He couldn't take it all in. He was confused and unreasonably happy. Should he feel joy or sorrow at knowing that he had siblings that he would never meet? His mother had given him a great and selfless gift, leaving him here to grow up an Apache man of the Tonto people. He wished he could thank her for that. He had his roots and his legacy, but he did not know his father's people or his mother and now he added three more relations to that list.

"I wish I could see them."

"Luke told me that you would ask that and told me to tell you that that is not possible."

"After all this time she still in danger?"

"Relocation is a permanent step, Jack. Once you go in, you don't come back. The Justice Department has never lost a single person who was relocated unless they broke cover. It's the single most dangerous thing your mother could do."

"A photo then," he said, knowing that a photo could be used to identify his family and therefore put them at risk. Even the simplest landmarks in a photo could reveal the part of the country and perhaps even the neighborhood where they lived.

Sophia did not directly deny his suggestion, but simply glanced away and then slipped back to her seat beside him.

Jack thought back to last February and remembered something. "When Carter had to leave us, my mother said something. It makes sense now."

"What did she say?"

Chapter Eighteen

Jack recalled exactly what his mother had said upon learning that Carter and Amber were being taken into witness protection. He repeated Annetta's words for Sophia now.

"She said, 'Not again.'"

Sophia cast him a puzzled look.

Jack explained. "She had already lost her sister to the Justice Department and she was about to lose her oldest son. Ironic. For a time she lost Carter and kept the son that was not hers."

"Jack, I've seen your mother with you. You *are* her son."

Jack bowed his head. He knew that was true.

His mother, Annetta, had never treated him any differently than the children she had had with Delane, except, perhaps, to minimize his concerns about how differently he looked than his brothers.

"You're right. Annetta has been a wonderful mother and Delane has been a doting father. I'm lucky. So why do I hurt inside?"

"I don't think you have to know your mother to miss her." Sophia cuddled up close to him on the sofa. She collected the hand he used to deform the sofa cushion beneath him and lifted it to give him a kiss on his knuckles. "Funny, you have two good women in your life. I'd be happy to just have one."

Jack had been so tied up with his own erratic feelings that he had forgotten Sophia's troubled childhood. He did not think to speak platitudes or trivialize her pain. But what could he say to comfort the woman who now comforted him?

"I'm sorry."

"Don't be. I'm lucky. I survived that and I'll survive leaving the Bureau."

"You have a home here for as long as you like."

She gazed up at him with a look of curiosity. Did she understand his invitation was personal and not a general announcement of the tribes' gratitude? He should make it clear that he wanted her to stay. But somehow the words failed him.

"Jack, there is one more thing that I learned from my cousin. It's also about your mother."

Oh, no, he thought, *she's ill.*

"Is she sick?"

"No," said Sophia, squeezing his arm and resting her chin on the top of his shoulder. "It's nothing like that. I'm just not sure how to, that is, I don't know how you'll take this."

He meant to tell her that whatever it was he could take it. But instead his mouth hung open and he waited as if he was a punch-drunk boxer unable to lift his arms to defend against the knockout blow. But he did see it coming. She had held it back perhaps deciding whether or not she should tell him.

"The Justice Department said she broke cover to come to Phoenix. As far as they could tell she never had contact with anyone from her tribe. They even checked the surveillance tapes to confirm she made no contact. In other words, she did not break the terms of her agreement. If she had, she would lose her status as a relocated witness. Just coming to Phoenix didn't do it. But it was close.

"She flew in and out on the same day. She was in the Phoenix airport for less than two hours. Surveillance tapes showed she did not speak to anyone other than the waitress who took her order. They checked on the waitress. She was not a relative."

"What was she doing here?"

"I think she was here to see you."

Sophia gave him the date of her breach of agreement. He recognized the month and date immediately and that he had been in Phoenix, in the airport at the same day and time.

"She came to see me."

"Yes. The Justice Department says your family was all there. Was that the day you came home from overseas?"

The closing of his throat hit him so hard and so fast that all he could do to answer her question was nod. He squeezed his eyes shut and felt the hot sting of tears roll down his cheeks. His mother had been there. Ava had seen him come off the plane. Drop his bag and hug his mother, father and two younger brothers. Carter had still been overseas, beginning his third tour. Jack had been certain after only one that the marines was not in his future. He had wanted only to come home to the place of his birth and return to the life he had left.

Sophia's arms went around him. She pressed her head to his chest as she continued to speak.

"She was at the gate directly behind the one

from which you disembarked and met your family."

Jack thought back to that day. Pictured her there across the wide polished floor, watching him greet the family she had given him. But unable to cross the few short steps to welcome him. Jack pressed a hand to his face as the sobs broke from his throat.

Sophia held on tight and cried with him. Her words were strangled but he still managed to understand past the sound of his own cries.

"It must've been the newspaper classifieds. Your mother, Annetta, must have posted the time and date of your homecoming."

Jack could only nod and sob.

Sophia stroked his arm and pressed a hand over his chest. She made soothing sounds in her throat and ran her fingers through his hair. Gradually the tension and pain drained away leaving him spent. He wiped the moisture from his face and blew out a breath.

"I haven't cried since Carter came home from overseas."

"It's cleansing, I think. Nature's way of helping us grieve."

Is that what he had been doing? Of course, she was right. He was grieving for his mother, Ava.

"I wish I could do the same and see them just once."

"I think if the Justice Department figures out what your aunt and mother are doing they might revoke her protected status. You would need to think long and hard about using the classifieds to arrange a meeting. It would be dangerous for her."

Jack let that wish die.

Sophia sidled forward until she sat on Jack's lap. She held his face between her two small hands and looked at him with a sweet expression of empathy.

Jack's heart still ached. But the pain was deeper now and mingled with joy. The dark

feelings that he had harbored about not belonging were gone. He did belong here on Turquoise Canyon. These were the people who
loved him and protected him and raised him.

"I'm a lucky man," he said.

"Yes. That's true."

They smiled at each other. Jack felt a rising
awareness of Sophia as she draped her arms
around his neck and her mouth turned upward
in an inviting smile.

"You hungry?" he asked.

Sophia shook her head, and her brows lifted
as she gave him an enigmatic smile.

"Thirsty?"

Another slow shake of the head.

"Sleepy?"

Sophia giggled. Jack stood, carrying Sophia
up with him. It was a short walk to the bedroom and the large welcoming bed. Jack did
not know if Sophia meant only to comfort him,
but he did know that for him this was so much
more. He had found another person that he did

not want to lose. Somehow, someway, Jack needed to keep Sophia with him. He began with soft, hot kisses to her neck and worked downward from there, each kiss a tribute.

Sometime in the night she roused him from his sleep stroking her leg along his as her fingers danced circles over his chest. He pulled her up so she straddled his hips, giving her leave to claim what she had summoned. This time was slow and quiet and joyful as Jack tried to show her what he could not yet say... *I love you.*

Afterward he held her as he slept, his slack fingers still tangled in her hair. It was there, naked and sated, that they still were when the siren sounded just after dawn.

Chapter Nineteen

Sophia scrambled out of bed first, pressing her hands to her ears as she tried to understand what was happening. The siren, it meant something. Jack sat up in bed, his eyes wide.

"The dam. Skeleton Cliff. That's the warning."

She knew it, of course, because she had heard it sound every day she was in range at noon. But that had been a short friendly toot. This was a shrill shrieking blast that went on and on.

"Dam breach," he shouted, leaping from bed and dragging on his clothing.

She glanced at the bedside clock. The time

read 5:51 a.m. Nearly everyone in Piñon Forks would be asleep.

Sophia scrambled to do the same, but he was already dressed and clipping his holster as she hopped on one foot in an attempt to tug on her second shoe.

Jack grabbed his phone and punched in a number, then frowned. He tried again.

Sophia had her holster on now and was dragging her hands through the tangle of her hair. She found the clip on the floor beside the bed and used it to hold back her long hair.

"What's wrong?" she asked.

Jack continued to jab at his phone. "No service."

An icy cold washed down her spine. She needed cell service to detonate the explosions. A terrible thought rose in her mind.

"Where is the cell-phone tower?" she asked.

Jack's eyes widened and she had her answer. She knew before he spoke, the flaw in their plan becoming obvious too late.

"It's right beside the power station at Skeleton Cliff Dam."

She made the obvious conclusion from the siren and the absent service. The dam was gone. Between the dam and Piñon Forks lay twenty-two miles and one bridge. How long until millions of gallons of water spilling from Twin Mountain Lake filled the canyon? How long until the hydraulic head, the wave of water, reached them?

"Jack. I need mobile service to trigger the fuses."

He stared at her and she could see the gasp, if not hear it. Then his jaw clamped shut and he pointed toward the door.

They ran to his SUV. Inside the compartment, the siren's wail was muted enough to be able to speak.

Jack lifted his radio and called in to the station. Somehow Chief Tinnin was already there.

"I radioed the highway patrol boys. The

dam's gone. Used a school bus full of something, they said."

"Kids?" she cried.

Jack relayed the question.

"They don't think so. Empty bus. They were expecting a field trip. Let it right by. And the two highway boys both got off the bridge before it collapsed."

Jack explained about the fuses.

"What do we do?" asked Tinnin.

"We need to get across the river," she said.

"A boat," said Jack. "Our patrol boat."

They reached the police station. Already the town of Piñon Forks was responding to the siren and everyone was attempting to reach higher ground, choking the narrow, poorly maintained road that was the single evacuation route from town. One of the tribal officers was directing traffic, but Sophia knew it would be too little, too late. The flood would find them here in their vehicles and everyone would become just part of the rolling, tumbling debris sweeping down the canyon. Unless she could stop it.

Sophia knew the main charges were all in place. But without the initiator, the cell-phone call, the detonator would not fire and the main charge would not explode. She needed another way to start the explosive chain reaction.

At the station, she collected the two rolls of a thousand feet of nonel shock tubing. This was her nonelectric initiator, a modern-day version of a burning fuse, replacing the iconic wires and TNT blast box. Only this was faster because the hollow tubing was coated with HMX, military-grade explosives that relayed the charge from the blasting cap to the det cord, which fired the main charge. With luck, this length of cord would give the distance they needed to protect them from the flying debris and blast wave. Her training had taught her that it was the blast wave that killed most people. She also gathered additional fifty-grain det cord just in case. Det cord, short for detonation cord, looked like shock-tubing cord. But it had a key difference. It did not transmit the blasting caps signal to the booster and explosives. It *was* the explosive. Wrap it around a tree trunk and bye-bye, tree.

Jack helped her carry the supplies to his SUV. They found that Wallace Tinnin was already at the river in the police boat that they used to patrol the portion of the river that adjoined their tribe's rez. The three of them loaded the blasting materials aboard.

Sophia climbed into the bow of the boat and sat facing Tinnin. He had a hold of the controls for the outboard motor and set them off the instant Jack had centered his body weight in the middle of the small craft, sitting on the white fiberglass livewell.

The chief ferried them straight across the river, but halfway to their destination the sirens went silent. The sound of the outboard motor filled the space as Jack and Sophia stared at one another.

"What happened to the siren?" asked Sophia.

"Not sure," said Jack.

"They could have taken that out, too," said the chief.

She had not thought of that.

"How long until it reaches us?" asked Tinnin.

"Depends on the size of the breach," said Sophia. If it was only a minor hole, the flooding would be minimal and the water would rise slowly. If the entire hydroelectric dam was gone…she couldn't imagine it. That huge grey structure, destroyed. But it could happen. Had happened to larger targets in military operations.

"I've had spotters from Tribal Thunder upriver since we identified the possible target," said Tinnin. "Today, it's Ray Strong. He radioed in. It's gone. Dam, power station—all of it."

And Ray's pregnant wife and Lisa were likely in the snarl of traffic in Piñon Forks.

Sophia felt the weight of their lives pressing down on her. They had to get to those detonators.

Jack and Tinnin stared at her as they jolted across the water—both seemed to be wondering if she could pull this off. She wondered with them.

"Okay." She turned her mind to the math problem. Water, volume and force. "The water from the lake will be forced through the gap in the dam. The flood will move outward as well as downriver. It has to fill up the canyon," she said. "There's a bridge between us and the dam site. That will slow the water and block the debris for a while. When it fails, the debris will be rolling toward us with the water in a wave."

"How long?" asked the chief again.

"Twenty minutes would be generous."

She needed to bypass to ignition sequences set with cell phones. That meant getting up close and personal. Way too close and much too personal with the amount of explosives lining that cliff wall. It also meant that both she and Jack would need to be in different locations to detonate the two respective sequences of charges she had laid.

She looked to Jack and his troubled eyes told her that he had already come to the same conclusion.

"How are we going to do it?" asked Jack.

Sophia wondered the same thing.

"We will each need to trigger one of the sequences. I'll take the first. You handle the second."

Jack's brow lifted as he seemed to realize that she had taken a more dangerous sequence.

"How about we reverse that. I'll take the first. You take the second."

"You can't." She was so glad to have a reason he would accept because she knew saying she needed to protect him would not fly. "I'll never scale that cliff face in time. And you've done it before." She pointed at the wall in question. The one he'd climbed as a young man. The first in his group to reach the top, he had said.

He could have driven upriver and over the bridge to reach the canyon ridge, if they had time. They didn't.

"We should stay together," he said, but he was accepting the truth. He needed to leave her to save his people. He didn't like it but could find no alternative. They would separate to initiate sequences or they would let the river take it all.

"How long will it take you to get up there?" she asked.

Jack considered the problem. Studying the route once taken by the ancient ones to the cliff dwellings in the caves she was about to destroy. These were left by the indigenous people who lived in this place far before the Apache moved over the land bridge with the Athabaskan peoples to this place. There were steps cut into the inclines to ease the way for the women who carried water vessels on their backs. On the steepest sections, the steps had been worn smooth by the rubbing of countless hands and feet of those who walked here before.

"How much will I be carrying?" asked Jack.

She organized what he would need as Wallace Tinnin opened the livewell, rummaging past their gear for the nylon bag that held survival equipment. He dumped the contents of the red nylon bag onto the deck and began loading up the blasting supplies she selected.

Sophia spoke quickly, feeling the pressure of time pushed by the oncoming water. Jack knew how to set the charges. He had been with her but still she reviewed how to use the detonator after the shock tubing.

"Get behind whatever you can. Something solid and as far back as possible. You need something to break the blast wave. Something solid and far back from the ridge."

He turned to go and then did an about-face.

Jack grabbed her wrist and tugged. Then he gave her a quick kiss and whispered, "Come back to me."

She nodded. Her throat was too full of pain and grief to answer.

The chief pressed a radio into her hand. "Tell us when you are clear."

Jack was already scaling the steps. She watched him a moment more and then turned to Tinnin.

"I might not have time to get clear."

He held her gaze. "Then radio us that you're clear anyway. He won't hit the initiator otherwise."

She understood. Telling Jack she was safe would ensure that he initiated his sequence.

Sophia clipped the radio to her waistband, scooped up the roll of shock tubing and took the seat vacated by Tinnin. Then she pointed the flat skiff upriver, toward her position.

In her plan, they would be across the river in cover when she made the two phone calls to the burner phones to trigger the blasts. Then she would blow the sequence upriver first, blocking the flow of the river. The second sequence would bring down more of the cliff above and reinforce the existing temporary dam. Without the second blast, she was certain the force of water would at least break over the smaller debris pile. At worst, it would take the pile of rubble and use it like a scouring pad to wipe away every structure and living thing along the river.

Unfortunately, after setting her sequence, she would have to travel above the range of the first blast site. She'd have to face the ensuing floods from the riverbank or she would have to race under the cliff face that was destined to fall in the second blast.

How much time had passed? Ten minutes? Fifteen? It would be a miracle to just get to the cell-phone initiator before the waters reached her. She glanced back, seeing Jack scaling the steepest section of rock with Tinnin still far behind him. They'd make it to their position and then it would be a race to lay out the tubing and take cover. They had a chance.

Sophia continued running along the flat riverbank, her gaze searching for the flood.

"Not yet. Please, not yet."

And then she saw it—the brown wave swept toward her from canyon wall to canyon wall.

Sophia reached the initiation site for the first blast and tied the tubing into the line she had set. Then she ran back toward the boat, unrolling the yellow tubing as she went. She threw the roll into the skiff and unrolled it into the river. Then she set the boat to drift. All the explosives were inside the tubing. It was waterproof, so no need to keep it dry.

Sophia glanced at the motor. If she engaged the motor, she could make a faster escape, outrun the cresting wave and possibly the debris from the second blast. But then the tubing might pull away from the initiator and there would be no first blast, no foundation for the second. Neither her sequence nor Jack's would provide enough of a debris field to hold back what was coming. They needed both. So she drifted along in the current, faster than normal in the swell of water already lifting the river's depth. As she went, she spooled out the tubing until she was directly beneath the site of Jack's sequence. Sophia glanced at the approaching hydraulic head, judging the speed and distance it covered. She wouldn't make it.

Then she lifted the radio. "Jack, over."

He answered immediately, out of breath. "Here. We're in place. Your position? Over."

"I'm initiating first sequence now. You're next. Over."

"Are you clear? Over."

"Clear. Jack, I see the flood. Initiate immediately after my blast. Over."

"Roger that."

Sophia couldn't save herself. But she could save Jack and all he loved.

She hit the trigger. The tubing flashed a brilliant white as it carried the signal back upriver. A moment later rocks and debris shot into the air as the canyon wall collapsed into the river.

Sophia hit the throttle and flew downriver, knowing she'd never make it to the still water she could see beyond the rock wall engineered to collapse.

Chapter Twenty

"She's done it."

Jack and Tinnin took cover behind the wall of rock at the top of the canyon rim. From this position he could not see the river directly below him. More importantly, he could not see Sophia. But he could see far upriver to the narrow gap between the walls of rock, and he could hear the echoes of the first blast rumbling through the stone beneath his feet as the dust billowed up into the blue sky.

If she'd calculated correctly, rock from the lower bluff should have collapsed into the river, blocking its normal flow. His sequence of blasts would bring down the overburden

Jenna Kernan 319

and cliff rim to fall on top of the first mound of rubble adding weight, depth and height to the new temporary debris dam.

"Hit the charge," said Tinnin.

Jack lifted the button. He needed only to press his thumb to send the canyon rim down into the river. But instead he held the control aloft and still, as if he, too, had turned to stone.

"Hit it!" yelled his chief.

"Hear that?" said Jack.

"What?"

"The motor. It's the skiff."

Jack dropped the control and stood. "She's not clear. She's still in that skiff."

"Maybe." Tinnin reached for the control and Jack snatched it back.

"She's under us! We have to give her time." If Tinnin thought to wrestle the control from Jack, he'd never make it. Jack faced his chief ready to fight to give Sophia the seconds she needed to escape.

But Wallace Tinnin did not lunge for the

control, or take a swing at Jack. Instead he pointed upriver. Jack stepped back, suspecting a trick, a diversion to distract his attention for the moment his chief needed to make a play. Then he glanced toward the gap in the canyon. What he saw frosted his heart.

Brown water roared through the opening, blasting forty feet to the top of the canyon walls. The hydraulic head—millions of gallons with only one way to go, straight at his reservation.

The anguish surged with the flood waters as he realized he faced a devil's choice. She could die in the blast or in the flood. He held the trigger in his hand and turned his gaze to his chief.

Tinnin lifted his chin, indicating the trigger. "That's quicker."

Jack turned back to watch the water. He could see pieces of metal in the debris field that Sophia had forewarned. Soon it would pummel everything below. Unless he stopped it.

He waited as long as he could, until the sound of the crashing wave drowned out the sound of her motor. Until the flood had reached the point where he could no longer see it run.

Jack pushed the trigger.

Tinnin jumped on top of him, upsetting his balance and forcing him back to cover. The earth beneath them heaved and groaned as the blast wave passed over them. Then the rock that had been there all Jack's life, and the lifetime of every person who'd ever walked the earth, dropped away. Where it had been was only dust and gravel and chunks of stone flying high, up and up.

"Get down," yelled Tinnin, pushing Jack's head to the warm sandstone.

All about them the rocks fell, raining down like a meteor shower. Mercifully, the debris missed their heads, which were pressed close to the outcropping they had chosen for cover. But one hit Tinnin's leg. He yelped and rolled from side to side as he clutched his thigh.

Jack checked his chief's leg. The deformity of the tibia and immediate swelling made it clear that both bones of his lower leg were fractured, and he could not walk down the way they had come.

"Call for help," said Tinnin. "Tell them I need transport."

Jack crouched beside his superior.

"I can't come with you, Jack. Go see if anyone is left down there."

Jack lifted the radio, issuing a prayer under his breath before pressing the button necessary to transmit. Please let his dispatcher be there. Please let everyone be there. Please let Sophia's death not have been in vain.

"Jack Bear Den, here. Are you there, Olivia?" Jack released the button and held his breath, waiting for their dispatcher to answer. As the seconds crawled by with the settling dust, Jack's heart beat so hard he could not swallow.

"They're not there," he said to Tinnin.

"Try again. She leaves that radio on her desk all the time."

"Olivia! Pick up! Are you there? Over."

The radio squealed and then Jack heard Olivia, out of breath.

"Yes. We're here. We're all here! I was at the window. I can't believe it. The rocks flew everywhere. It broke windows. But it worked. It stopped the water! Over!"

"Thank God," said another voice. Ray Strong, Jack recognized, who had spotted the flood from far upriver and whose new wife was there in Piñon Forks.

Jack pressed the radio to his chest and bowed his head to also give thanks. But the tear in his heart grew wider and he pressed his hand to his eyes. He wanted her back. He wanted to tell her that he loved her and that he was so sorry for what he had done to her. If not for him, she'd be back on the job she loved, alive.

Tinnin put a hand on Jack's shoulder.

"She's a hero, son."

He nodded and looked at the sky, still so filled with dust, it seemed like a cloudy day. He lifted the radio again and asked Olivia if she saw a boat on the river.

"A boat?"

"Our boat."

"Not from here. No, Jack."

"I see it." Another voice broke in. "It's Jake."

That was Jake Redhorse—one of their newest and most promising hires.

"I'm at the river. I see the boat. It's downstream on this side. Over."

"Where's Sophia? Over."

"Checking. Over."

Jack spoke to Olivia. He told her to call Kurt in Darabee and get the air ambulance ready.

"I'm not that hurt. It's just a busted leg," said Tinnin.

Jack glanced at his chief. "It's not for you."

Jack half expected him to tell him to give up. That all they'd find was Sophia's body, if that. But he couldn't give up.

"I'm going to the cliff edge. I'll be right back."

"Be careful," said Tinnin.

Jack crept forward. He crawled the last few feet on all fours until he got his head over the edge.

Below, a lake was forming behind the dam of canyon rock that Sophia had devised, the water threading up the box canyons and flowing out into the pastureland above the tribe's casino.

The river flowed in a fury, but it did not overflow the banks. He swept his eyes across the scene and found the fiberglass craft they had taken across the river together.

Why didn't you tell her you loved her?

He watched the patrol unit pull to the shoulder and saw Jake Redhorse jog down the bank. Jack looked downriver for her body, fearing he would see it floating in the current or worse, snagged on a log.

He saw nothing but the unusual brown muddy water. He returned his gaze to Redhorse, who searched the boat. From Jack's position, he could see the boat rested on its side against a large boulder. The contents of the craft were strewn along the bank. He looked again.

But the contents were all upstream from the boat. Wouldn't they be below the craft or in the river?

Instead he saw the life preservers, medical pack, flares and small shovel all thrown in a pile on the bank. It looked as if someone had dumped everything they routinely stored inside the fiberglass livewell onto the bank.

He looked at the boat's position again. It lay above the high-water mark. That meant it had been thrown up there or…

Could she have grounded the vessel? Sophia would know, or at least be able to guess, how far the rock would fly and how high the river would rise before they blocked the flow.

Jack lifted the radio. "Redhorse. Check the livewell!"

"The what?" Redhorse looked across the river and waved his arm above his head to show that he had spotted Jack.

"The bin where we stow that gear. Check it."

The livewell, designed to store large-mouthed bass on fishing trips, was also fiberglass, but Jack knew it had good insulation.

Redhorse affixed his radio to the front shirt pocket of his uniform and walked to the boat. The cooler was on its side. Redhorse lifted the two latches that locked when the lid dropped to the base.

Sophia spilled out onto the ground like a mermaid. She lay on the riverbank, motionless and pale.

Jack lifted the radio. "Is she breathing?"

Redhorse dropped to one knee and rolled Sophia to her back. Her arm flopped lifelessly above her head. The young officer lowered his ear to Sophia's lips and listened.

Jack spoke into the radio again. "Olivia.

Call Kurt. Send the air ambulance to your position now!"

Redhorse sealed his mouth around Sophia's and blew. Jack knew what it signified. Sophia was not breathing.

Chapter Twenty-One

Jack lay on his belly on the canyon rim staring back down to the river. The route down had vanished in the blast. The bridge above them was gone and he was stranded on the wrong side. He glanced across the water to see several people now gathering around Sophia, so many that he could not see her.

He prayed as he watched. His shaman had chosen the medicine wheel as Jack's guide. The circle of life and symbol of all things that were important. You knew they were important because they moved in a circle, like the sun and the seasons and the years in a man's life. Kenshaw Little Falcon said Jack would need to know the direction to go and the wheel would guide him. Four quarters, four directions and the fifth direction that was the place in the center.

He'd found his center. It was Sophia.

He'd found the direction he needed to go. Toward her and with her. If he had the chance, he would not let her go. He had done his duty to his people, the tribe of his mother. Now he would follow the hoop and the woman and ask her to pass through the circle of their lives together.

But first she had to live. She had to.

Jack studied the makeshift dam she had made. The temporary structure allowed natural spillways between the huge boulders and rubble that blocked its course.

Jack lifted the radio and hailed Jake Redhorse.

"Is she alive?"

Across the river, Redhorse stood holding the radio to his mouth. Jack could read nothing from his expression as he squeezed the radio so hard he feared it might crack.

"Affirmative. She's breathing. Over."

Jack closed his eyes and glanced up at the sky.

Thank you for this day and all that are in it. Thank you for her life.

Jack lifted the radio. "Get me down there, Jake. Get me to her. Over."

Olivia's voice broke in. "How's the chief?"

"He needs transport. His leg is busted."

The thumping of the helicopter blades flashed Jack back to Iraq, but he kept his attention on the group across the river. He knew it was the air ambulance.

"Jack, your brother is hailing me. Over. He wants to know where you want him."

"Set it down over there."

It seemed an eternity as he waited for Kurt to leap from the open door of the chopper and dart between the parting crowd to Sophia. He left her to fetch the stretcher. Jack knew that was good because his brother must have decided she needed nothing from him at the scene before transport.

"Is she critical? Over," he said.

"Negative. Coming around. Breathing. Good pulse, he says." Redhorse waved at Jack from across the way. "Kurt says they have time to land up there for the chief."

"Yes. Tell him yes." Sophia was loaded, Kurt disappeared aboard and the engine revved as the bird ascended. A moment later, Jack was shielding his eyes as dust and sand swirled beneath the landing chopper. The pilot set the runners on the plateau, where Chief Tinnin waited with Jack.

Jack ran to the open door as one of the crew emerged and ran past him with his bag. Jack wedged his shoulders past Kurt to get a look at Sophia. She was strapped onto one of two stretchers beneath a white sheet and her color was gray.

"How is she?"

Kurt rested a hand on Jack's shoulder. "You did it."

"Yeah." His attention remained on Sophia. "Is she all right?"

"I think that cooler protected her. But it locked on her. She ran out of air."

That was bad. Brain damage. Jack pressed his hand to his forehead.

"She's got good vitals, but she may have ruptured her spleen. Possible other damage—"

Jack cut him off. "Okay. Let's go."

Kurt slipped past him with the spine board and he and the other paramedic carried Tinnin to the chopper. Jack was already aboard.

"Aren't you in charge now?" asked Kurt, motioning his head to the tribe's side of the river.

"They'll have to wait."

Kurt's brows lifted in surprise. Then he took his seat and replaced the headset.

"Good to go," he said into the microphone.

The pilot gave a thumbs-up. The motor shrieked and then lifted into the air.

The canyon, the rubble dam and the river grew smaller and smaller and then fell away behind them. They landed in the parking lot beside the hospital in Darabee. Two teams awaited and buzzed forward, taking charge of the patients and leaving Jack with Kurt standing on hot pavement.

"Can you get me into the OR?" he asked.

"Not in a million years. Waiting room. Now I have to go back to work."

"Piñon Forks?"

"Minor injuries. We're taking the ambulances."

His brother left him and Jack headed inside. Over the next three hours, Carter called to update him on the tribe's status. Officer Redhorse called on the direction of the chief, who was already back in Piñon Forks. They were moving everyone to Turquoise Ridge temporarily, or out to Darabee. The FBI was on site and FEMA was coming in with temporary housing and still he heard nothing on Sophia's condition.

It was well into the evening before he received any news. The doctor met him in the waiting room, where Jack had about worn out the carpet pacing.

"How's she doing?"

SOPHIA FORCED HER eyes open and glanced about, struggling to figure out where she was. It didn't take a forensic explosives investigator to recognize she was in a hospital bed hooked to an IV, a finger monitor for her pulse and... She shifted, stifling a groan at the sharp abdominal pain and the tug that told her she was hooked to a catheter. She hated hospitals and instead of being glad to have somehow survived, she began immediately plotting her escape.

The room was dimly lit by the headboard light. The white curtain that circled her bed prevented her from seeing the window or, presumably, the second bed. *Night time*, she thought, and relaxed her head back onto the thin foam pillow.

She closed her eyes against the pain. Something was definitely wrong down there in her midsection. She moved her feet, grateful they were both there and still worked. Her hands balled into fists, minus the one encumbered by the dreaded finger clip. She turned her head, continuing her inventory, and spotted the call button looped around the raised side rail.

The sharp pain in her middle had morphed into a constant escalating throb that forced her to grit her teeth. The act of reaching for the button made her break out in a cold sweat.

What had happened to her?

Sophia pressed the button, which made a dinging sound. Something on the opposite side of her bed moved. She turned and saw Jack Bear Den lift his tousled head from the mattress beside her hip. His gaze was groggy from sleep.

"Sophia," he whispered, his tone echoing the relief that lifted his features. He straightened and she saw that he sat in an orange vinyl chair pulled close to her bedside in the dusty clothing he'd been wearing when she last saw him ascending that cliff.

"What time is it?" Her voice was a rustling thing, like dead leaves rattling in the wind. She pressed her dry lips together, realizing how much her throat hurt. That was very bad because it likely meant she'd needed a breathing tube and that meant either her heart had stopped or she'd had surgery.

Jack glanced at his phone. "Three in the morning."

"Which morning?"

"Wednesday."

"Lost the day," she said and gritted her teeth against the pain. Tears leaked from her eyes.

Jack stroked her forehead.

"You in pain?"

She nodded, eyes now squeezed shut. She had no energy left for words.

"I'll get someone." He rose and left her. She heard him meet the nurse outside the door and caught some of their conversation.

Then the nurse was standing on her opposite side offering soothing words and an injection in the backside. The relief was almost instant. But she also felt the world receding again and she did not know what happened. Had they done it? Had they saved his reservation and ended her career in two spectacular explosions?

JACK MET WITH Carter and Dylan and Ray in Sophia's hospital room that same Wednesday afternoon. They crept in trying not to wake Sophia.

"Sleeping?" whispered Carter.

"They gave her something for pain," said Jack. "She's out."

Ray, ever blunt, told him that he looked like he'd been blown off the mountain.

Dylan, ever the diplomat, asked how Sophia was doing.

"They took out her spleen. She lost a lot of blood from the rupture and they said she had at least one bruised kidney."

"In other words," said Carter, "she's lucky."

"And smart," said Dylan. "Using the livewell for cover. Brilliant."

"Nearly killed her," said Jack. "She ran out of air."

Ray was now peering at Sophia, as if judging her condition, and Jack had to resist the urge to shove him back.

"How's her…?" Ray pointed at his skull. "You know."

"No brain damage. Redhorse got to her fast enough." And for that he would be forever grateful. "She'll be fine in time."

"You hear back from her supervisor?" asked Carter.

"He'll be here soon. We need a plan. She saved us all and we need to be sure it doesn't cost her the job she loves."

"You said they ruled in her favor," said Ray.

Dylan turned to Ray. "He's not talking about the investigation. She just blew up the whole ridge. That's not what FBI agents do."

Jack could not have said it better. He knew what was most important to Sophia. It wasn't his tribe or the land. It was her career. She'd fought great odds to get clear of Black Mountain and make a fresh start. She was doing good work and if that was what made her happy, he was going to do everything he could to protect her from the fallout from their transgression.

"You have any ideas?" asked Carter.

Jack told him what he'd come up with. They added their opinions and suggestions on how to make the story believable. He hoped that they'd be ready when Burton and Forrest arrived with their posse of federal investigators.

They came to an agreement and stood ready to protect her from the FBI. Jack wished they were on their land as they would have a better chance of guarding her. But the FBI would not take a woman recovering from surgery from her hospital bed.

Would they?

Chapter Twenty-Two

Carter cleared his throat in that way he did to indicate serious matters. Jack glanced up from Sophia's pale face and gave his brother his attention.

"Mom asked me to give you this." Carter extended an envelope.

"You know what's inside."

Carter nodded once.

"What?"

"It's information on your grandparents. Your father's people."

Jack tore off the end of the envelope, drew out the page and flipped it open. Ray crowded in to read over his shoulder as Dylan and Carter waited for whatever Jack decided to share.

Ray pointed at the page. "How do you even pronounce that?"

"I don't know," said Jack, staring at the name of his father as he realized he was no longer roadrunner born of snake. He looked at the page. What clan was this? He read the names of his father written in Annetta's hand.

Hawaii
Keanae, Maui
Maua Kahauola (grandmother)
Clifford Taaga (grandfather)
Robert Taaga (father)

Jack glanced at Carter. "Mom said this is all her sister told her."

It was enough—the proper way to introduce a man beginning with the place of his birth, the names of his parents and finally the name of the man.

He tucked the page into his wallet, in the place where he had carried the results of the DNA test for eight months.

"Thank her for me."

Carter nodded.

"Why don't we wait out in the lounge for the agents?" asked Dylan.

Ray filed out of the room after Dylan, leaving Jack behind. The nurse bustled in and woke Sophia, then chased Jack from the room.

When he returned it was to find Sophia sitting up in the bed and looking more pale than before. The grayness of her complexion made the circles especially dark.

"You all right?" he asked.

BY ALL REPORTS, Sophia was healing, but she still felt mostly on the wrong side of terrible. Her nurse let her use the bathroom while Jack spoke to his medicine society in the hospital lounge. He stepped back into her room just after the lunch tray was delivered. The pain made her jaw lock and the welcoming smile felt forced.

His gaze swept over her. "You hurting?"

"They just gave me something," she said. "I will be dopey again soon."

But before they gave her the shot, they had tugged out her catheter and changed the dressings. Everything from her chest down was aching.

He kissed her forehead and she closed her eyes at the touch that was light and comforting. She was done here. The tribe was safe and her purpose complete. He didn't need her and she was free to go. But go to what? They'd ruled on her use of deadly force. Now she faced a new investigation over her actions. She had no defense. She would lose her job and her career. It mattered, but not as it had before. Was that because she knew she had done the right thing?

Jack pulled back.

"Burton is en route," he said.

She snorted. "Just when I thought I couldn't feel any worse."

"I'm going to tell them that you only advised the tribal council on how to remove dangerous overburden from the canyon rim."

"I blew up the whole canyon," she said. "Pressed the trigger."

"No. We blew it up. The tribe. All the miners of Turquoise Canyon will swear they set the charges."

"Under my supervision." She arched a brow, catching on to what he was attempting to do.

"Not according to them. They were removing overburden from the turquoise vein and added too much to the main charge."

"They are not going to believe that you set those charges off immediately after the dam failed."

"It didn't fail, Sophia. They blew it up."

"Who?"

"No one taking responsibility. Just like the pipelines in Phoenix. The FBI will question the timing. But our guys laid the explosives. They caused a landslide." He shrugged. "It happens."

He was offering her a way out. A way back to her position and her life. All she had to do was to go along with the cover-up.

"I can't, Jack."

"Well, I'm not letting you get arrested. You saved us, Sophia. Everything we have, we owe to you."

"No one held a gun to my head. I made the choice and I'll take the consequences."

"No. You won't."

"It was illegal."

"Kenshaw often says what is legal is not always right and what is right is not always legal."

She thought about that then said, "Convenient. Your shaman is a known member of the eco-extremists group."

"He also works with your agency."

"Jack. I blew up federal land. They're not going to ignore it."

"That's true," said a familiar voice from the doorway. "Might give you a medal for it, though."

Luke Forrest stepped into the room.

His confident smile waned when he took a good look at her. She had seen herself in the bathroom mirror when the nurse had forced her up. She thought that she would frighten small children in her current state. Grown men, too, it seemed.

"Oh, Sophia," he said and moved to the opposite side of the bed. "I'm so sorry."

"I'm alive. I'll be back on my feet soon."

"That's great news. Burton should be here soon. I wanted a chance to thank you and to apologize for putting you in this position."

She let him off the hook without regret. "I made my own decisions, Luke."

"But if not for me, you would never have been here."

"And everyone in Piñon Forks would be dead," said Jack.

She never would have met Jack. Her gaze flashed to him. He scooped up her hand. When she glanced back to her cousin, it was to see him looking at the place where their palms met and then back to her. His brow quirked as he likely connected the dots.

"Well, then. You'll be on disability for a while. After that, you planning on coming back to the Bureau?"

She looked from one man to the other, resisting the pull to stay here with Jack. What would that be like? Then she remembered, though he had extended the hospitality of his tribe, he had not asked her to stay with him. Had not asked for anything more permanent than sharing the time she had here. They'd gone in knowing she would leave.

But he was here with her in the hospital. Never left her side, judging from the dark stubble now growing on his face and the dusty clothing he still wore.

Did he want her to stay?

"You think they'll take me back?" she asked Luke.

"I think so. You not only saved this reservation, you kept that flood from taking out Red Rock Dam below the rez and possibly Mesa Salado Dam as well. If that had happened, we could have lost three of our four hydroelectric dams. The results would have crippled the electric grid. You did that, Sophia."

"She had help. If they're going to pin a criminal charge on her, then I have forty miners who will swear she advised against it."

"I think that won't be necessary," said Luke.

"They won't prosecute?" asked Jack.

"Can't guarantee. But I highly doubt it. You were on your land. Federal land, true. I think they'd be foolish to pursue a case. It would be nothing but bad press. But if they do, you'll need more than forty miners. The Bureau will know Sophia was there. She's left physical evidence. They'll find it."

Jack's grip on her hand tightened.

"You have a suggestion?"

"For starters, I'd move her out of Darabee and back to Turquoise Canyon. That would delay them. If she can travel, then consider taking her to her own reservation on Black Mountain. There are other ways to protect her."

Now he met Jack's gaze and Jack nodded.

"I understand."

She didn't. "What are you two talking about?"

Luke leaned down to kiss Sophia's cheek and whispered words of encouragement. Then he straightened and looked to Jack.

"You know what to do."

Chapter Twenty-Three

It was not how Sophia pictured being proposed to. She lay in a hospital bed hurting all over, a pulse monitor and IV connecting her to equipment beside her. In her mind's eye, her would-be groom would not have been rumpled and tired and covered with fallout from a recent explosion. And he would not have proposed to her out of duty and an obligation to protect.

Her mother's choices had taught Sophia many things. One was never to trust a man to take care of you. It was why Sophia needed her job. And no matter how much Jack tempted her, she was not putting her foot in that trap today or any day. One made decisions from a position of power, not from one of weakness, and she had never been so weak.

"No," she said and stopped talking.

Jack's brow furrowed. "But it would make you a member of the Turquoise Canyon tribe."

"I just blew up your canyon. You might need a new name. Turquoise Valley?"

"Sophia, this is serious. If you marry me, we can claim you have federal protection on our reservation."

"Jack, I'm Black Mountain Apache and I've spent my adult life trying to leave that legacy behind. But if I needed it, I have the protection of my tribe."

"You want me to bring you there?"

"No!" Oh, it hurt to raise her voice.

"Your captain will be here soon. I can have you out of here before he arrives."

"I don't need a husband, Jack. What I need is my old job back."

"Forrest thinks that might not work out."

"Well, I'm going to try. I'm sure not going to quit because they might fire me."

He blew out a breath. "Is that your decision?"

"Yes."

"You could come to work for us. We need more women on our force."

"You don't have any."

"Our dispatcher, Olivia. She's ten percent of our force," he said, rubbing his neck. "And she does a great job."

"I appreciate the offer. But I don't think you need a forensic explosives expert just yet. Maybe think about a second detective first."

"I don't want you hurt over this."

Did he mean more than a ruptured spleen and a bruised kidney? She was really tempted to just accept his offer. But she wouldn't. She wasn't going to be his act of selfless duty. No matter how good they were together, her ego could not tolerate that.

When her captain arrived with three investigators, they asked Jack to leave the room.

The last thing she said to him was to tell them the truth.

He was a lawman. But she feared that his need to protect her might make him forget that. It wasn't something you could do halfway. Either you followed the law or you didn't.

They asked her a series of questions, the interview stretching so long she feared she'd have to call for her pain medication. When they left, she felt totally drained. The medication helped her sleep. When she woke, Jack was back beside her bed.

"You don't have to stay. I'm doing well."

"I want to stay."

"Jack, go home. Take a shower. Sleep in your own bed and come back tomorrow."

"You ordering me out?"

"I need to rest."

He kissed her forehead and something unexpected happened. Despite the pain and fatigue, that familiar tingle of awareness was back. This man, only this man, could rouse her to want something her body was in no way ready for.

"I'll see you in the morning," he promised and disappeared.

She ate and slept and watched television with the sound off, dozing and waking to find the windows dark.

In the morning, her breakfast came, but Jack did not. She tried to hide her disappointment and worry.

That afternoon, Executive Director Gill of the Turquoise Canyon tribe came to her room dressed in full regalia to formally thank her for her efforts to save their tribe. Chief Wallace Tinnin accompanied him, on crutches, his leg in a cast from hip to toe. Also there were the members of Tribal Thunder—Ray Strong, Dylan Tehauno, and Carter and Jack Bear Den.

Jack looked especially appealing in his high beaded moccasins, bright camp shirt festooned with blue ribbons sewn horizontally across the yoke. Across his forehead he wore a red band of folded cloth ornamented with a string of silver and turquoise medallions on a leather cord. Two eagle feathers hung by his temple. His appearance was so distracting that she had to concentrate not to keep staring at him. Each time she cast him a quick look, her stomach gave a familiar quiver. Perhaps she was healing faster than she thought.

The tribe presented her with a sacred eagle feather adorned with red cloth and elaborate bead work and a simple leather cord to allow the feather to be tied on whatever she chose. The eagle flew closer to the heavens than any other creature and was therefore the most sacred. She had earned one such feather before from a bald eagle presented by her tribal leaders to mark the milestone of graduating from high school. The entire brief ceremony at her bedside made her proud and she accepted the golden eagle feather with two open hands from Executive Director Gill. The feather, a symbol of strength and power, was holy to her people. There was no higher honor and she felt humble indeed.

"You are one of us now," said Gill. "And welcome on our land and in our homes. Know that we are forever grateful."

"I'm honored."

The room seemed very empty after they left. She had come to know them. What would it be like to stay here with them?

The longing welled up inside her. She sat with the feather before her on her lap, bright against the white blankets. Then she lowered her head and wept. She didn't want to leave them. She didn't want to leave Jack. But how could she stay?

He had so much work to do with his tribe and with the FBI, who were now investigating the dam explosion and the secondary blast that saved his reservation. She had no right to detain him when she was healing well. They needed him, she didn't. Only she did and that was the most concerning thing of all.

The nurse surprised her a few minutes later. Sophia swiped away the tears.

"Well, they're finally gone," said her nurse, clipboard firmly gripped in her hand. She spotted the feather. "Isn't that pretty."

"Sacred," she said, correcting the woman.

The nurse shrugged. "I have your discharge papers."

Sophia blinked. She had been told she would be released tomorrow and the switch caught her by surprise.

"Oh, well, that's good."

"Someone has to pick you up. Do you have someone to call?"

Jack, she thought.

"Um, yes. Of course." It was in that moment that Sophia realized that she had the FBI, an office, a job and coworkers. But she did not have a friend to call to come get her or a family member ready to drop everything to drive her from Darabee to Flagstaff. Suddenly her career seemed cold company by comparison to the warmth of Jack Bear Den's arms.

She lifted her mobile, called her office and asked for her captain.

"I was just going to call you. How you feeling?"

"They're releasing me. I need a ride."

"I'll send someone. Listen. We have good news."

She could use some. "What's that?"

"The ballistics came back on Jauquin Nequam's rifle. It's a match for the bullet fished out of Bear Den's vehicle."

"Great."

"We have him in custody. I've met with Mr. Nequam. He's removed the hit order as part of a plea."

Sophia bristled. She didn't want him getting off after taking a shot at her.

"Really?"

Burton might have heard the aggravation in her voice.

"Sophia, he fired at the highway patrol and fled the scene before arrest. We got enough on him. He's not getting out."

"That's good. How's the highway patrol guy?"

"He didn't hit him," said Burton. "I understand the shooter put a hole in his hat. But he's fine and his hat is in an evidence locker."

"Any progress on the dam explosion?" she asked.

"Lots. Listen, I've got to go. We have a driver on route. Should be there soon."

She thanked him but he'd already ended the call.

Sophia dressed in the clothing Jack had brought her from his apartment. Then she added the eagle feather in its presentation box to the top of her overnight bag. But she paused before closing the bag, retrieving the feather and tying it in her hair.

Sophia was done pretending she was other than what she was. She was Apache, Black Mountain tribe, and she would not let her mother's bad choices keep her from claiming her heritage.

She tried not to be disappointed that Jack did not appear to say farewell and resisted the urge to call him to tell him of her early discharge. Instead, she waited on her bed until a stranger from the Bureau appeared at her door, presented his ID and walked beside the wheelchair she was required to use. On the ground floor, she could not keep herself from searching the lobby for Jack, as if wishing would conjure him. If she wanted to say goodbye, she should have called him.

But she didn't want to say goodbye and that was exactly the problem.

JACK HEADED FOR the station after another sixteen-hour day. He had never been so busy or so distracted. He knew from Forrest that Sophia had been discharged and had been back on the job for eleven days. Everything was as it had been. He had his work. She had hers. That was what she wanted, wasn't it?

He knew she didn't want him. He'd not said a formal goodbye to her. But he had asked her to marry him and she'd turned him down. He'd seen her at the feather ceremony. It had been very hard not to linger after the tribal representative had left. Not to grovel and beg her to come back.

He placed a hand over the medicine wheel he wore around his neck and felt the presence of the one upon his back as he wondered what direction to go.

His shaman said he needed the hoop to help him find his path. When the temporary dam was shorn up and the FBI finished with their investigation, perhaps he would take a trip to Hawaii to find his father's people, see the land where Robert Taaga had come from and learn exactly how to pronounce his grandmother's name. He imagined flying to Maui with Sophia and frowned.

Jack pulled into the lot at tribal headquarters and stared across the river at the dam Sophia had built them in two separate blasts. The woman knew her business. He was on dry ground now only because of her.

Repairs were underway for the damage resulting from the blast. There had been few injuries, which was miracle enough.

Jack headed in and checked his messages. There was nothing from Sophia and the rest could wait. He was expected at his parents for supper. Sunday again.

He was the last to arrive as it was after eight. But they had waited. Tommy was back home because of Jack's urgent call for help after the dam's destruction, but his brother would be returning to the border tomorrow. So this was a final chance for the Bear Den boys to share a meal until they gathered again for Christmas. Carter and Amber greeted him at the door. He kissed his mother in the kitchen and they all came together at the round, scarred wooden table that showed the marks of having survived the raising of four boys.

Jack enjoyed the company as much as the food. He was starving, having missed lunch again. His mother commented that he was losing weight. He usually just wasn't hungry anymore.

"Any word from Sophia?" asked Carter.

The table went silent as all eyes turned to him.

He shook his head and pushed the remains of the noodle casserole around his plate.

"That's odd," said his mother, her brow furrowing.

"Anything from Forrest on those responsible?" asked his father.

His mother made a sound of frustration and stood to clear the table. Amber and Carter helped her carry out the dishes.

"They're collecting evidence. I understand they have the school bus, or what's left of it."

"What about Lupe Wrangler?" asked Carter. "They going to extradite her?"

"According to Forrest, she has family in Mexico and they still have not broken her alibi for her husband's murder."

"So she gets away with it?"

"They are making progress and they've locked up her money. That's all I know."

His mother called from the kitchen. "Jack, come help me with this."

All eyes flicked to him. Tommy gave him that you're-in-trouble look and lifted an index finger. Carter grimaced and Kurt rubbed his face. Every last one of them knew he was being summoned, and not to help in the kitchen.

His father rose. "Boys, it's a lovely night. Let's get a fire started out back."

Jack's father was abandoning him and taking all Jack's backup along. He pressed his hands on the table and rose to face the music.

Chapter Twenty-Four

"You going to read me my rights first?" he asked, folding his arms across his chest and staring at his mother.

"What?" she asked. Her mask of innocence did not fool him for one second.

"You know, my right to remain silent?"

"Don't be silly. I want to hear about Sophia. Why haven't you called her or gone to check on her? Isn't she still under a hit or something?"

"Removed. She's safe."

"So you think she doesn't need you. Is that it?"

"No. Yes." Jack flapped his arms. He was used to being the one doing the interrogation.

"Jack Bear Den, I saw the way you looked at that girl. And I saw the way she looked at you. She's beautiful, smart, serious, works in law enforcement, so she'll understand the ridiculous hours you keep. Is it because she's Mountain Apache?"

"Is what because she's Mountain Apache?"

"That you're letting her go. Because, if you want my opinion, she's in love with you."

"You're wrong there," he said, unable to keep the edge from his voice.

His mother thrust a fist to her fleshy hip and lowered her chin. Jack's ears went back as he recognized the signs indicating he should take cover. Instead he dug his hole even deeper.

"Mom, Sophia doesn't want to stay up here in the pines with us Tonto Apache." There had been long-standing animosity between the Western Apache and his people and it was easier to blame that than voice his confusion.

Her mouth dropped open but she rallied. "It's because you're Tonto? I don't believe it."

"I don't know." He rubbed his neck. "I was just supposed to escort her and protect her while she was here. She's gone now." He flapped his arms.

"I see that. I just don't understand it. Did you tell her your feelings for her?"

"Of course I did. I even asked her to marry me."

His mother's eyes rounded and he thought she might be beginning to understand that Sophia had left him and he was doing his best to get over it…and failing.

"You asked her?"

"I just said so."

"With a ring?"

"What?"

"Did you have a ring? Did you get down on one knee like your father and beg her to marry you?"

Jack scowled. "No, of course not."

His mother was now staring at the ceiling

as if counting to ten. When her eyes met his, her brows were up and her chin down again.

"What did you say, exactly?"

Now he was looking away. "I don't remember."

She placed a hand on his folded arms. "Jack?"

"I said that if she married me, she'd gain tribal protection against federal prosecution. That I could marry her and the tribe would keep her safe."

"How romantic."

"I was offering to be her husband."

His mother shook her head in a way that signified either disappointment or that he'd blown it somehow. He thought the latter but wasn't quite sure. He shifted from side to side and her hand squeezed his arm, bringing him back to stillness.

"You offered," his mother said. "You didn't ask."

"Mom, she said she didn't need a husband. She needed her job back."

"You made her feel like an obligation. Do you love her?"

"Of course."

"Start with that."

"That's stupid," he said.

"Why? Because you will have to wear that heart of yours on your sleeve instead of keeping it trapped in that big barrel of a chest? That's the point, Jack. You have to take a risk to show her that you can't live without her. You have to say the words and hope she doesn't turn you down. You offered a plea bargain, not a proposal."

Had he? He swiped a hand over his mouth.

"Try again, Jack, and bring the biggest diamond ring you can afford."

SOPHIA HEADED FOR the break room to freshen up her coffee. She had been riding a desk for two weeks. She didn't like it, watching the other agents in her office come and go as she remained behind with the paperwork. Her captain did a much better job at keeping her informed. The official line was that her little round of private explosives were counterterror measures taken by the Turquoise Canyon tribe in conjunction with federal authorities. That sounded so much better than rogue agent. She was under the impression that they'd keep her awhile and fire her when the media coverage petered out. Her union rep and their attorney suggested she get a deal in writing and get out while the getting was good. But where and to what? She thought of Turquoise Canyon and grimaced. The canyon was much wider now and the US Army Corps of Engineers was working up there.

She wanted to call Jack and see how he was doing. Busy, of course. She wondered about Federal Agent Cassidy Cosen. She knew the Anglo had married tribal councilman Clyne Cosen, but what did she do, commute from way up there on Black Mountain all the way down to Phoenix every day?

Logistics. That was not what was keeping her from Jack. It was stubbornness and fear. Stubbornness that he wanted to protect her instead of love her all her life. And fear that if she took him up on the offer to protect her, she'd lose the control she'd gained over her life.

"That's why they call it falling," she muttered.

Like a trust fall, you had to take a risk.

"Knock, knock." She knew the voice without looking up. It was one of the agents in the office, Patrick Gaffney.

She plastered a smile on her face and turned toward Patrick. Why was he verbally knock-knocking on the open break-room door?

"You busy?" he asked.

She shook her head.

"I brought you a visitor." His expression was entirely too manic for the generally taciturn agent.

"Yeah?"

Normally, they went out to meet visitors and did not bring them back to the break room. She had a sudden terror that it was her mother. Sophia set down her mug on the table.

Patrick stepped aside and Jack Bear Den filled the doorway. Patrick poked his head up from behind Jack's shoulder like a prairie dog emerging from his burrow.

"I'll leave you to it," said Patrick and he disappeared.

Jack stood with his hat in his hand. Sophia sucked in a breath as her heart began a jolting beat that made her eardrums pound. It was hard not to rush forward and leap into his arms. How she wanted to do just that. Instead she casually reached for a chair back for support, fumbling her grip. She got a tight hold on the second try and she allowed her gaze to sweep over him, searching for changes.

His attire was more formal than usual.

He wore lean jeans. Beneath the cuff poked large, elaborately tooled boots she had never seen. The leather was obviously gator and some of the stitching and accent pieces were turquoise in color. His belt she recalled, staring for a moment at the familiar enameled buckle—the medicine wheel to help him find which way to go.

Had it led him here?

There was a visitor's pass stuck to the lapel of his gray sports coat. Around his neck hung a necklace of disc-shaped turquoise beads holding a medallion featuring a large piece of turquoise framed by two bear claws set in silver. The ornament was bright against his white cotton shirt. Jack had dressed in his best.

She lifted her gaze to his familiar face. He was clean shaven and his chin dipped as he peered at her from beneath a hooded brow.

"Sophia," he said. "I've missed you."

Her heart continued its silly pounding. She licked her lower lip and saw his gaze drop to her mouth. Now the pounding moved south and her grip on the chair back tightened.

"This is a surprise," she said.

"A happy one, I hope." He cleared the doorway and she saw he carried a bouquet of red roses mingled with baby's breath. The paper-cone wrapping was crushed tight in his fist as he held the flowers upright like an ice-cream cone. "I brought you these."

Red roses. A dozen, at least.

Her gaze flicked to them and back to him as she tried to interpret the gesture. These were not the sort of flowers a man brought a woman in the hospital or to congratulate or to thank. He knew that, right?

"You look well," he said.

She didn't, but the cover-up helped disguise the circles and weight loss, which she blamed on the surgery.

He continued forward, stiffly, as if his boots hurt his feet. His finger slipped under the collar of his buttoned shirt and tugged. There was sweat on his upper lip.

Now, she had seen Jack in situations that

should have made him sweat. Under fire in his SUV. Helping her lay det cord on the canyon and flying across the river in a boat to reroute the explosive series. He had not ever looked this nervous.

"What are you doing here, Jack?"

"Came down to ask you a question."

A question or *the* question?

"These are for you." He approached, arm extended as he thrust the flowers at her.

She collected the bouquet and inhaled the floral perfume. "Thank you."

At first she thought he was bowing because his head inclined. But then she realized he was kneeling. Jack sank to one knee before her and fished in his pocket.

Sophia stopped breathing.

"SOPHIA?" JACK SAID. His mouth was so dry it tasted like sand.

The darn box wouldn't open. He pulled and realized too late that he had it backward, as the tiny hinge came apart and the top section dangled like a bird's broken wing. He scowled at the damaged black velvet. The slot still held the white gold band set with a low-profile solitaire.

He held out the offering.

"Sophia, I'm in love with you. I want you to be my wife."

Her mouth dropped open and her eyes went wide as she looked at the ring and the box with the dangling top.

He rushed on, trying to assure her. He knew her feelings about commitment and relying on a man to provide for her.

"I want a partner, Sophia. I want you as my partner. You might not believe me, but I will always protect you and provide for you. But I don't expect you to give up anything. I want to join your life, not take it over. Will you at least consider me as a husband?"

Her mouth closed and her chin began trembling. He hadn't seen this before. Should he stand up now and gather her in his arms, or just stay here holding out the ring?

Sophia set the roses on the table and reached, placing her hands on his extended one. She was nodding frantically as if she had suddenly lost the ability to speak.

"Is that yes?" he asked.

"Yes," she squeaked.

He blasted forward like a center tackle coming off the line at the snap and pulled Sophia to his chest. She hugged him around the neck, and he inhaled the sweet familiar scent of her.

How he had missed her. Suddenly everything seemed just right. He set her on her feet and pulled the ring from the slot.

She smiled up at him as he held the tiny ring between them. She gazed down at the glittering ornament.

"The guy said he could size it to fit or that you can return this one and pick something you like better."

She wiped the tears from her cheeks and

glanced down at the engagement ring. "I couldn't like anything better than this one."

Sophia offered her left hand and he slipped the circlet to her knuckle. She took it from there, sliding the ring down her slim finger and into place. She took a moment to admire the setting, smiling down. Then she lifted her gaze to meet his.

"I never thought I'd want this," she said.

"I always wanted this," he said. "I just never thought I'd find the right woman. But I have found her in you." He took her left hand in his, picturing the wedding vows and knowing they could not come soon enough. "I'm sorry about the first time I asked you. It was stupid. I made it sound like I was doing you a favor because I was afraid of doing this." He lifted her left hand.

"Asking me?"

"You told me flat out that you would never depend on a man."

"I did say that."

"I think it's just smart to be in control of your life, Sophia. I understand that and only want to be with you, always."

"I love you, Jack. You make me want to believe. You're worth the risk."

He dragged her in for another hug and then a kiss and then another. When they finally came up for air, Sophia giggled and cried all at once.

"I want a honeymoon," she said.

"All right. Where to?" he asked.

"Hawaii."

Now Jack's mouth dropped open as his breath caught.

"I want you to find your father's people, Jack. We'll go together. I'll help you."

"'I'll help you,'" he repeated on a whisper. "Those might be words as important as 'I love you.'"

"What about my job?" she asked.

"I'd never ask you to leave your work, Sophia. It's important, what we do. The world needs protectors."

She smiled up at him and in her sparkling eyes he could see a brave woman, a survivor and a life mate who would walk with him on the journey of their lives. Jack had finally found his direction and his true path, here with Sophia.

* * * * *

MILLS & BOON®
Large Print – July 2017

ROMANCE

Secrets of a Billionaire's Mistress	Sharon Kendrick
Claimed for the De Carrillo Twins	Abby Green
The Innocent's Secret Baby	Carol Marinelli
The Temporary Mrs Marchetti	Melanie Milburne
A Debt Paid in the Marriage Bed	Jennifer Hayward
The Sicilian's Defiant Virgin	Susan Stephens
Pursued by the Desert Prince	Dani Collins
Return of Her Italian Duke	Rebecca Winters
The Millionaire's Royal Rescue	Jennifer Faye
Proposal for the Wedding Planner	Sophie Pembroke
A Bride for the Brooding Boss	Bella Bucannon

HISTORICAL

Surrender to the Marquess	Louise Allen
Heiress on the Run	Laura Martin
Convenient Proposal to the Lady	Julia Justiss
Waltzing with the Earl	Catherine Tinley
At the Warrior's Mercy	Denise Lynn

MEDICAL

Falling for Her Wounded Hero	Marion Lennox
The Surgeon's Baby Surprise	Charlotte Hawkes
Santiago's Convenient Fiancée	Annie O'Neil
Alejandro's Sexy Secret	Amy Ruttan
The Doctor's Diamond Proposal	Annie Claydon
Weekend with the Best Man	Leah Martyn

0617 GEN STD LP

MILLS & BOON®
Hardback – August 2017

ROMANCE

An Heir Made in the Marriage Bed	Anne Mather
The Prince's Stolen Virgin	Maisey Yates
Protecting His Defiant Innocent	Michelle Smart
Pregnant at Acosta's Demand	Maya Blake
The Secret He Must Claim	Chantelle Shaw
Carrying the Spaniard's Child	Jennie Lucas
A Ring for the Greek's Baby	Melanie Milburne
Bought for the Billionaire's Revenge	Clare Connelly
The Runaway Bride and the Billionaire	Kate Hardy
The Boss's Fake Fiancée	Susan Meier
The Millionaire's Redemption	Therese Beharrie
Captivated by the Enigmatic Tycoon	Bella Bucannon
Tempted by the Bridesmaid	Annie O'Neil
Claiming His Pregnant Princess	Annie O'Neil
A Miracle for the Baby Doctor	Meredith Webber
Stolen Kisses with Her Boss	Susan Carlisle
Encounter with a Commanding Officer	Charlotte Hawkes
Rebel Doc on Her Doorstep	Lucy Ryder
The CEO's Nanny Affair	Joss Wood
Tempted by the Wrong Twin	Rachel Bailey